SILVER CITY SCANDAL

BY THE SAME AUTHOR

GERALD HAMMOND

SILVER CITY SCANDAL

St. Martin's Press
New York

444398

Library of Congress Cataloging in Publication Data

Hammond, Gerald.
  Silver city scandal.

  I. Title.
PR6058.A55456S5 1986   823'.914   86-11909
ISBN 0-312-72588-4

First published in Great Britain by Macmillan London Limited.

First U.S. Edition

10 9 8 7 6 5 4 3 2 1

SILVER CITY SCANDAL

ONE

Aberdeen Sheriff Court is not usually a welcoming haven, but Keith Calder was thankful to find its shelter. The north wind had made a right-angled turn at the Citadel and was whooping along Union Street with the gusto of a small boy pursuing a puppy.

An elderly official directed him to the witness room, which he found to be empty except for a mousy girl with a file of papers and a harassed expression.

'At last!' she said.

Keith did not suppose that she had been impatient for his manly charms. She would, undoubtedly, be from the office of the Procurator Fiscal. 'In point of fact,' he said, 'I'm early.'

'But the High Court's getting ahead of itself. Some of the cross-examinations took half the expected time. I don't know why you couldn't have been available from the start of the trial like other witnesses,' she finished peevishly.

'My hourly rate seemed to put you off,' Keith said.

'That's another thing. There's a set daily rate for witnesses.'

'Which would buy my time for about ten minutes a day,' Keith said. He was both bored and amused. He had given evidence often in the past and had had the same conversation almost as often. 'Take it to the taxing master if you like. He'll only agree with me.'

The girl flushed. Keith guessed that she was a recent graduate from law school, feeling her way. 'But we

5

only want you to confirm the sale of a gun,' she said, pouting. 'Nothing difficult.'

'That doesn't make it less important,' Keith pointed out. 'This is a case of murder, unless the local fuzz have been pulling my leg. And it doesn't make my time any less valuable.'

The girl was prepared for further argument, to which, Keith decided, he would reply with sarcasm. She was mildly attractive when she remembered not to glower, but no sexual vibrations were passing between them. They were saved from a downright explosion by a voice in the corridor.

'Christ!' she said. 'They want you. You're sure you know what to do?'

Keith lost patience. 'Since before you were born,' he said.

Pink and fuming, she led him out. The macer took over and brought him into Aberdeen's largest court-room, in temporary use by the High Court. Keith took his place on the witness stand, very conscious of the low, wooden canopy over his head, designed to throw the sound of his voice to the jury who were packed into their cattle stall opposite him. At his side was the shorthand writer, and beyond her the judge whom Keith knew to be Lord Aberford. Out of the corner of his eye Keith could see the dock with the public benches and gallery beyond, but he avoided looking in that direction. He had been called by the prosecution and any sympathetic eye contact with the accused might dent his impartiality.

Lord Aberford rose to administer the oath and then lowered his stout, elderly body back into its ornate chair with a satisfied grunt. The witness, as always, was left standing, perhaps as a reminder to be short-winded.

The Advocate-Depute rose from his seat at the crowded table below the judge's bench and glanced at his brief.

6

'You are Keith Calder?' he began.

Keith agreed.

'Please tell the court your occupation.'

Keith thought that a modicum of advertising never came amiss. 'I am a gunsmith,' he said, 'and a dealer in good quality new and used shotguns and rifles and in antique arms. I also act as a shooting instructor. I have a shop in the town of Newton Lauder, Borders Region.'

He would have gone on to mention dog training and to extol the quality of his fishing tackle, but the Advocate-Depute broke in.

'I hand you this book. Please tell the court what it is.'

Keith took the large, cardboard-covered notebook into his hands. 'This is one of a series of similar books in which I keep the record, required by the law, of guns bought and sold. It covers a period of some eight months, roughly five years ago.'

'Please open the book at the marker and look at the entry at the top of the right-hand page. From that entry, what can you tell the court about the transaction?'

Keith looked down at the book although he already knew the entry by heart. The Newton Lauder police had visited him on several occasions and had taken more statements from him about that entry than he cared to remember.

'On the eighteenth of November, almost exactly five years ago,' he said, 'I sold a new, Spanish, sidelock, twelve-bore shotgun, number two-five-three-four, made by Armas Alicante. For business reasons, certain details of stock dimensions and choke borings are also noted. The purchaser produced a shotgun certificate, number five-three-three-one, which gave his name as Hugh Michael Donald and his address as Ingoldsby Drive, Aberdeen. The price is also recorded.'

The Advocate-Depute had run out of questions. But he was uncomfortably aware that a costly error had been made in fetching an expensive witness half the length of Scotland while the defence might not have objected to the introduction of Keith's records by a police witness. He knew it to be a cardinal rule never to ask a question in direct examination to which the answer is not already known. But the Advocate-Depute made a mistake. He decided to ask a question to which he thought that the answer was obvious.

He caught the macer's eye. 'Would this be the shotgun referred to?' he asked.

Keith, also, was aware that he had hardly justified his fee and expenses. He was, moreover, irritated that the girl from the Procurator Fiscal's office should have thought him unworthy of his usual fee. He glanced down at the gun which the macer had handed him. 'I can't possibly tell you that,' he heard himself saying.

There was a gentle stirring in the courtroom. The Advocate-Depute swallowed, audibly. But it was too late to retreat. 'Does the number correspond with that in your records?' he asked carefully.

Keith removed the fore-end, opened the gun and read the number on the action. 'It does.'

'And am I not right in thinking that no two similar guns ever bear the same number?'

'You are not,' Keith said. He was beginning to enjoy himself. 'I recently saw two Luger pistols with identical numbers. Luger ran two series of numbers, one for military productions and another for pistols made for the civilian market.'

'But. . . .' The Advocate-Depute paused for a second's thought. 'There would be no military production of shotguns?'

'I would suppose not,' Keith said. 'Certainly not of sporting sidelocks.'

'Then can you suggest why Messrs Armas Alicante should duplicate numbers?'

'I can,' Keith said. 'The firm was long-established,

8

but you will note that the number of this gun is low, which suggests that the firm started a fresh series of numbers with each model. This particular model was aimed at the British and similar markets and it may be that a separate series of numbers was used for export guns as against those for sale at home – differentiated, perhaps, by the size or style of numbers. Only reference to the firm's records would determine whether that's so. And I'm afraid that the firm went out of business shortly after this gun was made. Their records may be unavailable.'

If the Advocate-Depute had not known that he had already done more than enough damage, the expression on the Crown Office solicitor's face would have told him. He decided to wind up his examination without giving the defence any more straws to grasp. 'Does this gun appear to be of the make, model, style and type which you sold and which is recorded in your book of records?'

'It does,' Keith said.

'And the arrival in this country of a similar gun bearing the same number would be highly improbable?'

'It would,' Keith agreed.

'Thank you. I have no more questions for this witness.'

The Advocate-Depute sat down and tried to ignore what the Crown Office solicitor was whispering at him.

Counsel for the Defence rose, an elderly man, his age accentuated by his grey wig. His eyes were friendly but abstracted. He had been given one unexpected card to play in an otherwise hopeless hand.

'Mr Calder,' he began. 'You say that it is possible – unlikely but possible – for two guns such as the one in your hands, and similarly numbered, to have reached this country. Is that right?'

'Yes.'

9

In for a penny, Counsel thought, in for a pound. 'Please look at the defendant,' he said. 'Is that the man to whom you sold this or a similar gun, five years ago?'

Keith looked at the defendant for the first time. Flanked by two strapping policemen he looked small, although he was of burly build. He had a round face and his very black hair was repeated on the backs of his hands and in the blue of his chin. Keith liked him on sight and thought that here was a man from whom he would buy a gun unseen. This was Keith's highest accolade. Counsel for the Defence had looked similarly trustworthy, whereas Keith had already decided that, if he should ever buy anything from the Advocate-Depute, he would count his change. Out of such small things grow greater decisions. Keith would help the defence if he could.

'After five years,' he said truthfully, 'I've no recollection at all. I certainly don't remember seeing him before.' He gave the advocate a meaning look and willed him to go on.

'What you are saying is that you can not in all honesty swear that you sold this gun to this man?'

'That's true,' Keith said. He repeated the look.

Counsel hesitated and then decided to plunge. 'Would it surprise you to know that, while the defendant admits to having bought a gun from you of that make and pattern and to having used it regularly for the intervening years, he will emphatically deny that this is the gun?'

'Not in the least,' Keith said.

The public benches, which were three-quarters filled, were unnaturally silent. Not a cough, not even a loud breath could be heard. Something new was coming.

'Please tell the court why not.'

Keith suppressed a smile. The door was open. 'This gun wouldn't fit the defendant,' he said. 'A shotgun isn't sighted like a rifle. Its accuracy depends on its being

10

fitted to the user, so that when it's correctly held and his cheekbone is on the comb – the top – of the stock, his eye is aligned with the rib. There are exceptions to that, but it is generally true. The gun must also be the right length for the user. For that reason, standard guns as mass-produced tend only to suit men of average build and are often altered to fit users who differ from the norm. I do a lot of that sort of work.

'The defendant,' Keith went happily on, watching from the corner of his eye the consternation developing at the prosecution's half of the table below him, 'seems to be smaller than average but heavily-built and with a full face. If I were altering this gun to fit him, I would expect to shorten the stock, perhaps giving the butt a slight forward angle so that recoil wouldn't bruise his rather deep chest. And I think that he would need the cast – that's to say the horizontal bend in the stock – to be increased to allow for the squareness of his jaw.

'But this gun has actually been lengthened by the addition of a rubber recoil-pad and the stock has been straightened to remove the slight cast which it would have had as standard.' Keith stopped and looked Counsel in the eye.

'Would you care,' Counsel asked hesitantly, 'to suggest the build of the owner of this gun?'

'Tall and thin,' Keith said. 'Quite possibly left-handed.'

'I'm very much obliged to you,' Counsel said. He looked at Keith without receiving any more signals. 'No further questions,' he said.

There was a subdued buzz of comment in the courtroom. As the Advocate-Depute rose to his feet, it died away.

'Your Lordship will appreciate that some of this witness's evidence was unexpected. Might I request an adjournment while this aspect of the case is examined,

11

and to take further instructions?'

Lord Aberford was not noted for his indulgence when Counsel found themselves in difficulties. 'You might make such a request,' he said, 'but it would not be granted. Mr Calder is your own witness, and it is neither the fault of the court nor of the defence if you were inadequately briefed. However, we will adjourn for lunch now and resume at two p.m., which allows you a few extra minutes. I take it that you have not finished with the witness?'

'Indeed I have not,' the Advocate-Depute said grimly.

'Very well. Be back here at two o'clock,' Lord Aberford told Keith. 'And you are not to discuss your evidence with anybody. Anybody at all,' he added, in the direction of the Advocate-Depute.

Keith crossed Union Street through the first flurry of snowflakes and treated himself to lunch at the Athenaeum. He was back in the courtroom by the appointed hour. On the way, he crossed with Counsel for the Defence who looked at him hungrily but turned away.

Court re-convened. The Advocate-Depute rose to re-examine. He looked like thunder – Keith suspected that he had missed his lunch – but his manner was more sorrowful than angry.

'Under cross-examination, Mr Calder, you made statements which were not in your precognition. Why were we not given the benefit of your – shall I say? – theories in advance?'

'I was not shown the accused or the gun,' Keith said, 'or I would have pointed out the incompatibility between them.'

'Ah, yes. This alleged incompatibility.' The Advocate-Depute tried to sound as if he were enjoying

12

himself. 'Thank you for reminding me. Are you saying that this man could not have shot with this gun?'

'No,' Keith said, 'I'm not. I'm saying that he would have missed to the left, or would have found himself very much better at targets which crossed from right to left than vice versa; which for all I know was the case. And I'm suggesting that no competent gunsmith would have made these alterations to this gun for this man.'

The Advocate-Depute glanced down at a page of hastily scribbled notes. 'But am I not correct in thinking that a perfectly competent gunsmith will sometimes, on his own suggestion or that of a shooting coach such as yourself, alter a gun in a way that might appear abnormal, in order to compensate for an habitual error on the part of the owner? In other words, that the alteration in question might have been made in order to cure a habit on the part of the defendant of missing on the right?'

Keith decided that the Advocate-Depute had not sacrificed his lunch in vain, and he wondered which local gunsmith had been dragged away from his own meal. 'I wouldn't consider it good practice unless there were a physical infirmity causing the problem,' he said. 'It's much better to make the gun fit the man properly and then teach him to shoot straight with it.'

'But it does happen?'

'Regrettably, yes.'

'And at the hands of perfectly competent gunsmiths?'

'Occasionally,' Keith said.

'So your earlier comment was erroneous?'

'Certainly not.'

'I put it to you . . .'

Lord Aberford leaned forward. 'You must not cross-examine your own witness,' he said with relish.

The Advocate-Depute sighed. He looked hard at his notes and then sat down.

Keith looked hard at Defence Counsel, who rose but then hesitated and studied his own notes before speaking.

'My learned friend has been referring to the – ah – bending of the stock of the gun. Forgive me if my grasp of the technical expressions is less than adequate. But what opinion do you have regarding the lengthening of the stock? Would a competent gunsmith have carried out such work for the defendant?'

'Not even an incompetent gunsmith,' Keith said, 'would suggest lengthening a standard stock to suit a smaller than average man.'

'Thank you very much indeed.'

Both Counsel indicated that they were finished with the witness and Keith was allowed to stand down. Two separate discussions, whispered yet of evident urgency, were in train at the advocates' table.

Having put the cat among the pigeons, Keith would have liked to remain and observe the feathers flying. But his evidence had only been expected to last for a few minutes, and as a result he was already overdue to meet his wife. He left a note with the macer for the defence solicitor, donned his sheepskin coat and made his way back, through falling snow, to Gregor's Hotel. The wind had dropped. The streets were wet with grey slush, but the snow lay clean in Union Terrace Gardens and the noise of the traffic was muffled.

TWO

Keith found his wife enjoying the luxury of afternoon tea in the hotel's broad lounge and watching the comings and goings of the oilmen and their women. They exchanged affectionate glances, which were all the greeting needed between them. Keith lowered himself stiffly into a seat beside her.

'Any tea left?' he asked.

Molly poured tea while embarking on an account of her day. Keith waited patiently. He had long since learned that her attention would be elsewhere until she had recounted, in strict chronological order, all that she had done, whom she had met, who had said what and why, and what she thought about it all. Molly, for her part, had learned not to expect her husband to chatter unless he were in a talkative mood or had a message to impart. They no longer tried to change each other's habits. Perhaps, Keith thought, that is what love really is.

She ran down at last. 'How did you get on?' she asked.

'Fine.'

'You didn't say anything rude?' Keith had been known, when deeply immersed in his evidence, to lapse into broad Scots or, worse, into vulgar vernacular.

'I watched my tongue,' he said. 'You could have taken me for a professor from St Andrews. All the same, I dropped a bomb on them,' he added with relish.

'How?' Molly demanded. 'What did you do? I

15

thought you only had to speak to the shop's records about a gun we'd sold.'

'That's right. But they showed me the gun and they showed me the accused who was supposed to have bought it. The gun had been altered, and no way would it have fitted him. And I told them how similar guns can sometimes turn up with the same numbers.'

'But, Keith, when those two Lugers showed up, you said that it was as rare as a new star in the east.'

'I told them that it would be unusual but possible. They can make what they like of it.'

'Wasn't it the same gun, then?'

'Probably. How would I know? It may have been through a dozen pairs of hands and been altered to fit every one of them. I wouldn't have rocked the boat at all if some young quine from the Fiscal's office hadn't got uppity about my fee and expenses. And now, I suppose, they'll refuse to pay them and Wallace will have kittens.'

'Oh, I wish I'd been there, but it didn't sound as if it was going to be interesting. So what happened after that?' Molly asked.

'I haven't the faintest idea. They'd finished with me, the room was cold, my feet were wet, the public benches looked about as comfortable as kirk pews and I was late for meeting you. So I left a note for the defence solicitor, just in case they want to call me for their own side, and buggered off.'

Molly heaved a sigh for Keith's unnatural lack of curiosity. 'Do you think they will call you?'

'Shouldn't think so. The prosecution were hindered because the judge wouldn't let them cross-examine their own witness. But if I turn up for the defence, they can make me qualify most of what I said until there's hardly anything left. American style gun-fitting and a gun that shot low and so on.'

16

'So we still go home tomorrow?'

'Probably. But if this snow keeps up I don't know that we'll fancy the drive. Now, let's go up, bath and get changed ready for dinner.'

'Don't rush me,' Molly said. 'I'm enjoying myself.'

Keith was still soaking away his stiffness in a hot bath when he heard the room telephone buzz apologetically. Molly, who was already half-dressed, took the call.

'Reception says that there are two men wanting to see you,' she said through the open door.

'Say that we'll be down in a whilie. We'll meet them in the lounge.'

Molly relayed the message, listened for a few moments and then hung up. 'They'll be waiting in the lounge bar,' she said. 'Would they be the defence lawyers, or somebody angry from the Fiscal's office?'

'The defence,' Keith said. 'The Fiscal may want to have words with me, but he wouldn't suggest meeting me in the bar.'

'Can I come along too?'

'I don't see why not. I've nothing to say that you won't be able to read in tomorrow's papers.'

The Calders made their entry into the lounge bar some three-quarters of an hour later. Keith was no more than clean and tidy, but Molly dazzled. She had made an effort. She was old-fashioned enough to consider lawyers, along with doctors and ministers, to be a cut above the rest, two steps below the aristocracy but only one below God.

Keith had no difficulty in recognising the defence solicitor who had been at Counsel's table in the courtroom – an untidy man with thinning, red hair and a face which seemed to have been assembled clumsily from perfectly good components.

17

'Good of you to meet us, Mr Calder,' the solicitor said. 'I'm Jeremy Prather. And you almost met Mr Donald a little earlier in the day.'

For the first time, and with a sense of disbelief, Keith realised that the other man was the defendant whom he had last seen looking small but lost between two policemen in the dock. He managed to find words to introduce Molly.

Prather beamed at her and straightened his grubby tie. 'Drinks first,' he said, 'and explanations to follow.'

The solicitor's pint glass was almost empty and he treated himself to a refill. Keith took a large malt whisky, Molly a gin and tonic. Hugh Donald accepted another small sherry. Prather led them to a corner table where some potted plants would screen them from the occasional curious glances which Donald was attracting from the other drinkers, and lit a cigarette.

'Your evidence,' he said, 'was supposed to be the drawstring which pulled the prosecution's case together. Renfield, the Advocate-Depute, dried up. Our advocate, John Jenkins, wanted to go to the jury without putting on any case at all. I thought that he was taking a hell of a risk but, as he whispered to me, putting Hugh in the box would have given Renfield a chance to make him look a liar about the gun, among other things, on cross-examination. And if we called you as our witness, he could have torn you apart.' (Keith winked at Molly.) 'So up he got and pointed out that it was for the prosecution to prove their case. Since they had manifestly failed to do so, he said, he did not feel called upon to present a defence.

'Renfield tried to repair the damage in his closing speech and probably made bad worse. Lord Aberford, who never has any sympathy for an advocate who cocks up his case, summed up, mostly in our favour, and directed the jury, all in fewer words than I'd have

18

believed possible. I hear that he has a new mistress back in Edinburgh, so maybe he was in a hurry to get home.

'The jury were only out for about five minutes before they came back with a unanimous verdict.'

'Not guilty?' Molly suggested.

'There's the rub,' Hugh Donald said glumly. 'Not proven. Which isn't quite the same thing.'

'Not by a hell of a long chalk,' Prather said.

A waiter arrived, bringing menus, and asked whether they intended to dine in the hotel.

'My instructions are quite clear,' Prather said. 'I'm to invite you to dine with us. You're included, of course, Mrs Calder. This is both a celebration and a conference.'

'Does Mr Donald issue even his dinner invitations through his solicitor?' Molly asked curiously.

'The invitation is not Mr Donald's. It comes from his boss, Jonas Horseburgh, the managing director of Shennilco.' From Prather's tone, Keith guessed that if the solicitor had been wearing a hat he would have removed it before mentioning the name.

'Very kind of Mr Horseburgh,' Keith said. He caught Molly's eye. She nodded happily.

They ordered, without regard to the prices in the right-hand column. Prather ordered wine. The waiter promised to call them as soon as their table was ready.

'More drinks?' Prather said. His glass and Keith's were empty, but Molly and Hugh Donald had hardly begun on theirs.

'My turn,' Keith said.

'Certainly not. When the Old Man says "Pay for everything", I wouldn't dare to disobey.'

'Leave me out, this time,' Hugh Donald said. 'My head's unaccustomed to high living.'

Prather went up to the bar, lighting his third cigarette of the evening and dropping ash down his already disreputable suit. He seemed to be on friendly terms with the barmaid.

'So you're with Shennilco,' Molly said. 'That's an oil company, isn't it?'

'One of the biggest in the exploration field,' Hugh Donald said.

'Is Mr Prather with Shennilco too?'

Mr Donald shook his head. He looked mildly offended at the suggestion that his company might have on its staff anyone as scruffy as the solicitor. 'He's in practice in the city. A one-man-band. He turned up a fraud against the company in the course of his other business, took it to the Old Man and handled his end of it very discreetly. Since then, we've used him from time to time. Not on major legal matters, unless you'd call my problems that. The Old Man likes to use him as a sort of agent in the field. And I must admit that he usually gets results. Not this time, though.'

'At least you're out,' Molly said. 'And here.'

'Thanks mostly to your husband. You were quite right about the gun,' he said to Keith. He looked up as Prather returned carrying a tray with four fresh glasses. 'I did say that I'd sit this one out,' he added mildly.

'Don't drink it if you don't want to,' Prather said. 'But there's a company car coming for us, so you can get stoned if you like. God knows I would, after three months in the pokey.'

'It's all been too quick,' Hugh Donald said. 'I don't feel ready yet to put another layer of unreality on top of what I've already got.'

'You were saying about the gun,' Keith reminded him.

'I did have it shortened to fit me better. But I had a recoil-pad fitted at the same time. So when the police asked me whether the gun they showed me was mine, I said at first that it was. But then it struck me that it looked . . . different.'

'Longer?' Keith asked.

20

'Perhaps. If they'd put it into my hands, I'd have known. But what I most remember is a feeling that the figuring of the walnut stock looked different – I couldn't have said in what way – and that the gun looked tattier and more second-hand than I remembered,' Donald said. 'I expect you know how it is with something you've used for years without really seeing it any more. It just looked unfamiliar. So I changed my mind and told the police that it wasn't my gun after all, in spite of the number. Which didn't do my credibility any good,' he added.

Keith looked at Prather. 'Couldn't the gunsmith who altered the gun have been called?' he asked.

Prather shook his head. 'Before I got to him, there was a fire in his shop. By the time his stock of cartridges and powders had gone up, there wasn't much left of the shop, let alone the records. He thought that he remembered doing the job for Hugh, but it was more than four years ago and he'd never have stood up to cross-examination.'

'Well, I think that's a bit too much coincidence,' Molly said. 'Especially when you remember that something else funny was going on.'

'I thought so too,' Prather said. 'So I asked Hugh how many people knew that that gunsmith had worked on his gun.'

'And I told him,' Donald said, 'that almost everybody knew it. We do a lot of entertaining in the oil industry and Shennilco runs a shoot on Deeside. One of my jobs is to entertain any business contact who fancies a day's shooting, so whenever anybody needed work done on his gun I'd recommend this chap and show them my stock as an example of his work.' His expressive features suggested that he was a natural smiler. In court he had looked nervous. Meeting the Calders, he had looked tired. But, suddenly, he looked appalled. 'Don't tell me that I brought disaster down on him!'

21

'It was always a possibility,' Prather said. 'It didn't lead anywhere. The fire officer couldn't rule out arson, but suspected an electrical fault.'

'You never told me any of this. You just said that he couldn't back me up.'

'No point adding to your worries,' Prather said. 'Here's the waiter. Shall we take these up with us?'

In the dining room, inelegantly art nouveau compared to the mahoganied opulence of the lounge and bars, Prather had arranged, again, for a table with some privacy. They talked on as the courses came and went and the wine disappeared, halting only when a waiter was at the table and the subject was confidential.

Over the onion soup, Prather managed to find a gap in Molly's gentle prattle. 'You'd better explain the problem,' he told Hugh Donald.

'The problem's this,' Donald said. 'I'm a senior executive with Shennilco. Supplies manager to be precise. Which means that I have to make personal contact with a great many people, all well up the ladder. And, what's more, it means that I have to be trusted.

'I was accused of a crime, and a particularly nasty one in the public mind – shooting a relatively harmless woman because she was a nuisance to me. I hope I don't have to say more than that I didn't do it. The evidence was circumstantial—'

'Most evidence is circumstantial,' Prather put in.

'—but it looked bad until you, Mr Calder, came along and made a hole in the middle of it. Rightly or wrongly, my Counsel decided to go to the jury without putting on a defence.'

'You didn't have one,' said Prather.

'Let me tell it, all right?' Hugh Donald asked irritably. He flushed, conspicuously against his prison pallor. 'Sorry. Put it down to the strain. And so, the jury bring in a verdict of not proven. Which really means, "We

22

think you did it, but they haven't proved it, so don't do it again."

'Well, that's no good to me, or to Shennilco. I can't do my job while I'm tainted by having what is almost a conviction and admonition hanging over me. My depute's been carrying on for me, but for the last few months the work has been routine. Now there are some big deals in the offing which can't wait much longer, and he just doesn't have the weight for them. I have to get back on the job immediately if not sooner, and without a stain on my character. But my lawyers tell me that there are no legal steps to be taken.'

'My dear lad,' Prather said unhappily, 'even if you could get the case re-opened, which you couldn't, the verdict might just as easily be changed the wrong way as the right one.'

'My only escape,' Donald said, 'is for the real culprit to be found and convicted. That's all,' he added bitterly.

'More to the point,' Prather said, 'that's what the Old Man wants. And what the Old Man wants, he's inclined to get. The police won't want to touch it with the proverbial barge pole and I've already shot my bolt, quite apart from having a modicum of work of my own to be getting on with.

'So I'm to ask you whether you'd undertake an investigation for us.'

Keith had seen the proposal coming and was not enthusiastic. Aberdeen in mid-winter had never been among his favourite haunts, and since the arrival of oil had brought with it soaring prices, an influx of many nations and traffic congestion, he liked it less. 'Why me?' he asked plaintively.

'I know it may seem unusual. . . .'

'It's not all that unusual,' Keith said. 'Until the thirties, when the first police laboratories were set up, all scientific work was handled by independent experts.

23

In England, Robert Churchill and Major Burrard shared all ballistic and firearms work. Nowadays, of course, the police labs do all the work for the prosecution, but the defence can only turn to freelances like me. But why not somebody who knows the local scene?'

'Nobody leaps to mind,' Prather said. 'But, more to the point, you've had a good press recently for beating the police to the punch and coming up with real answers.'

'Mostly because of local knowledge. Those cases have been nearer home.'

Hugh Donald pushed his plate away, still half full. 'This afternoon wasn't local knowledge,' he said.

'This afternoon was pure bloody mischief,' Keith said.

'But it will bring more publicity,' Prather pointed out. 'Local publicity. And that's exactly what we need. The first thing is to show Hugh up as obviously wronged. The Old Man wants the Shennilco PR Department to get maximum mileage out of Hugh's determination to clear his name and Shennilco's confidence that he can do it.'

The idea of working in a glare of publicity horrified Keith although he could understand the need. 'I simply don't have the local knowledge—'

'I can obtain it,' Prather said.

'—office facilities—'

'Share mine.'

'—and I'd need a full-time dogsbody to sift and file and phone—'

'There's my cousin Sheila,' Molly said suddenly. 'She was a personal secretary until the firm moved away last month. And she speaks Spanish, if you wanted somebody to phone Spain and find out about the numbers. I think you should take it on, Keith. Wallace won't mind looking after the firm again as long as you're bringing in your fees.'

'As to that,' Prather said, 'you can regard money as the least of the problems. Shennilco is right behind this, and if there's one thing I've learned about the oil industry it's that the throughput of money is so colossal that a million or two can get lost as petty cash. So there'd be no difficulty, for instance, in offering a reward for information. And I think that they could afford to spring us another bottle.' He emptied the survivor into his own glass and made signals to the wine waiter.

'And you could get Ronnie to come and help,' Molly said.

'I suppose so,' Keith said. Molly's brother, a professional stalker, had his uses; but it was Keith's private opinion that, apart from his skill as a tracker, Ronnie's most useful function would be for shoring up a wall.

He toyed with his glass while he thought about it. Keith had, on occasions, worked for clients with almost unlimited resources and had found the experience rewarding. But another objection was looming. 'You want publicity,' he said. 'But, if Mr Donald is innocent, somebody else is guilty. You're going to tell him that I'm coming after him. And I've had my family threatened before now, when I was getting too close on somebody's tail. Molly, if I take this on you'll have to take Deborah with you and go to your Auntie Annie in Dunoon.' This was a private code for Keith's sister in Aberfeldy.

'All right,' Molly said.

'You'd better phone Wal. He can put Deborah on the train in the morning. You take the car and meet her at Dundee.'

'There's no need for Mrs Calder to drive,' Prather said. 'A company car, with driver, can take her anywhere she wants to go.'

'Will the roads be passable?' Molly asked.

'Good point. I'll find out whether one of the company

25

choppers is free. It can take you to fetch your daughter, and on to Dunoon or wherever you want to go.'

'It must be confidential,' Keith said.

'It will be,' Hugh Donald said. 'Our pilots get paid not to talk.'

Molly was beaming. Her few previous jaunts by helicopter had been hugely enjoyed, her pleasure being marred only by the fact that her daughter had not been along to share it. Keith was less happy. The safety record of oil company helicopters was less than perfect. But he could see that objection would be useless.

'That's settled then,' Prather said happily. 'I think our minds are too full for any more discussion tonight. Conference in my office tomorrow morning?'

'All right,' Keith said. 'I'll want to see the transcripts of the trial and all the precognitions. Bring any diaries, game books and so on for the period when you bought the gun,' he told Donald, 'and again for the time of the murder. Nine a.m.?'

Jeremy Prather shuddered ostentatiously. 'Legal diaries don't have any spaces before ten,' he said.

'Ten, then?'

'I suppose so.'

Hugh Donald had finished his main course and refused a sweet. 'I've always been an early riser and an early bedder,' he said, 'and prison hasn't changed my habits. Also, I've got to settle back into my flat. You'll excuse me?' he asked Molly.

Molly graciously agreed.

'I won't wait for the company car, then. I'll get a cab. Ten, tomorrow.'

With Hugh Donald's disapproving presence removed, Jeremy Prather settled down to serious enjoyment of Shennilco's hospitality. The Calders lagged far behind him, and when Prather hailed a friend they made it an excuse to escape to their room.

'Why did you want to wish your cousin Sheila onto me?' Keith asked as he undressed.

'She's efficient and she's available,' Molly said. 'You don't realise the job you'd have finding somebody like that in Aberdeen these days.'

'Is she as big a chatterbox in Spanish as she is in English?'

'Oh, Keith, she isn't a chatterbox. Just because she doesn't mind passing on news of the family . . .'

'Compared to you, she's silent as the grave,' Keith said.

To prove him wrong, Molly held her tongue for almost a minute. 'How much would Hugh Donald be earning?' she asked suddenly.

'At a guess, between sixty and eighty thousand,' Keith said. 'And most of it probably guarded against tax. They pay their big men enough to keep them honest. Why?'

'I just wondered. According to the papers, he's a widower,' Molly added, with apparent inconsequence.

'You just wondered whether he'd make a good husband for your cousin Sheila. So that's what you're up to!'

He turned, intending to give his wife a reproving look and a lecture about matchmaking. But Molly, in her thirties, had matured from a pretty girl into a very beautiful woman. Reduced to a gossamer pair of pink panties, she looked . . . delicious. And they were about to be parted.

Keith pounced. Molly squeaked and pretended to struggle.

THREE

In the morning, Keith saw Molly leave for Dyce Airport in a luxurious Jaguar emblazoned with the Shennilco insignia. Jeremy Prather might not accord with Molly's idea of a solicitor (Keith was experienced enough to be less sanguine) but at least he was as good as his word.

Keith walked up Union Street and, not for the first time, regretted how the Silver City had changed. Banks and insurance companies seemed to have squeezed most of the shops out of the city's centre and the traffic was now heavy and cut-throat with drivers chasing the oily dollar. The snow had stopped and the streets were swept but the temperature remained below freezing. A thin sun had broken through, and in the clear air it seemed that he could see each speck of quartz in the granite fronts shining a hundred yards away.

Jeremy Prather's office in Chapel Street was in a converted, two-roomed flat over a dry cleaner. Keith was early but the solicitor arrived on his heels and let him in, dumping a bundle of papers on a cluttered desk.

'The final transcripts,' he said. 'I had to go and fetch them myself, at this ungodly hour.'

'You poor sod.' Looking again at Prather, Keith realised that the description was apt. The solicitor was clearly hung over. 'Leave me to read them over. You go and get a hot bath, shave and change into something a little cleaner and dressier. We wouldn't want Molly's cousin telling her that you received us in that state, would we?'

'Why would she mention a thing like that?'

'I don't know why,' Keith said, 'but she undoubtedly would. Can I use your tape-recorder?'

'Help yourself. I think I'll do as you say. Not to impress your wife's cousin, but it might make me feel a little more human. I shan't be long. I have the flat upstairs.' He shambled out onto the stairway.

Keith looked around. The office had once been somebody's parlour and was still papered with faded roses. The carpet was threadbare, the furniture dilapidated. But, courtesy, presumably, of Shennilco, the business equipment was the latest and best.

He moved a hard chair to the window and began to read. He was an adept speed-reader and made quick progress. From time to time he dictated notes into Prather's tape-recorder.

The opening speeches provided nothing of relevance and he skipped to the evidence of the witnesses. The story began on the first of September, with the discovery, by one William McKillop, a farmer, of the body of a woman on his land near Kemnay, ten miles north-west of Aberdeen. The witness had earlier heard two shots, some seconds apart, at about seven a.m.

The corpse had been identified as having once been Mary Mae Spalding, a spinster aged thirty-six, who lived with a friend, also female, in a bungalow half a mile away. The late Miss Spalding had been a chartered accountant, a partner in the firm of Haydock, James and Spalding of Aberdeen.

A pathologist had examined the body and clothing. He put the time of death at early that morning, perhaps seven a.m. Death had been caused by gunshot wounds, specifically number six shot from a twelve-bore shotgun fired from close range. (Keith smiled. Defending

29

Counsel had picked the good doctor up sharply as to how he had determined that the shot had been fired from a gun of that bore. The doctor had admitted drawing an inference from the presence of a twelve-bore gun nearby. But the count of 302 pellets had agreed with the average for a standard twelve-bore cartridge and number six shot.) A rabbit, found nearby, had also succumbed to number six shot. The woman's body was suitably dressed for a walk on a mild but cool morning. The clothing had not been disarranged and there was no sign of sexual interference.

Well, that was a relief.

A twelve-bore shotgun had been found near the body. One barrel had been discharged. The police laboratory had been thorough. The firing-pin and extractor marks on the discharged cartridge had been matched to the gun. The shot and the wad recovered from the body, and the shot from the rabbit, had been compared to those in other cartridges of the same, very common, brand and found to be identical. Ownership of the shotgun had been traced to the accused through the records of the dealer, who would be called later.

Hugh Donald had been interviewed and later charged. After being cautioned, he had admitted being in dispute with the deceased. He could hardly have done otherwise. During the summer, he had applied to the Sheriff Court for an interdict restraining Miss Spalding from following him around while he was shooting on that land, disturbing his quarry and making the successful pursuit of rabbits or woodpigeon impossible. Support from the farmer being tepid, the application had been refused. He had absolutely denied being on the land that morning and claimed that he had visited the foreshore near Ellon, but no witnesses could be found to support that claim.

The accused also insisted that he had had his gun with

him that morning but had returned it to his flat before going to work. The same evening, he had reported to his local police station that his home had been broken into during the day and his gun stolen. He had seemed uncertain of its number and had only furnished it the following day, allegedly after making reference to his insurers.

The accused had refused to make any further statements to the police, presumably having obtained legal advice. And, Keith thought, about time too.

But two witnesses had come forward, neither of them damning but each adding a scrap of doubt to the scales. One, whose bedroom window overlooked the field-gate where Hugh Donald habitually parked his car, was sure that a car of similar size and colour had been there that morning, although under cross-examination had proved to be less than certain of the day. The other, while cycling to work, had seen a man in the distance dressed much as Hugh Donald was wont to dress and walking away from the place where Miss Spalding had later been found. Although he had been too far off to be sure that the figure resembled the accused physically, he thought that the man had not been carrying a gun.

The police had made a thorough search of the area for a considerable distance around the body. Several trivia traceable to the defendant had been found, not surprisingly when it was remembered that he had been shooting regularly over the land. But the significance of one such item had probably, Keith thought, accounted for the jury's verdict of not proven rather than not guilty. This had been Hugh Donald's cheque book, containing the stub of a cheque which he had written in a hotel late the previous evening.

That had been all the hard evidence on the prosecution's side. But it had been enough. Keith decided that only his own evidence about the gun had saved Hugh

Donald from a worse verdict than not proven.

The only precognition which seemed to be on hand was that of Hugh Donald. Keith was about to skim through it when he was interrupted by the arrival of Donald himself, accompanied by two springer spaniels of the short-nosed working style. The dogs seemed remarkably well trained; at no more than a flick of their master's finger they lay down under a corner table never moving but watching him with eager eyes.

'Sorry if I'm late,' Donald said. He took the other hard chair. A night in his own bed seemed to have relaxed him and he even managed a pleasant smile. 'I collected the hounds from the kennels, and they were in sore need of exercise and a little discipline. So I've walked them round half the city. Prather can't complain. A little dog hair can only improve this slum. I suppose he's still in bed?'

'He's up, but he's gone back to smarten up a bit,' Keith said. He nodded at the dogs. 'Nice pair. You trained them yourself?'

'From six weeks old.'

'And you shoot rabbits over them, using both dogs together?'

'Usually.'

Keith revised his opinion of Hugh Donald. Although he had liked his cast of features he had also wondered whether to agree with Jeremy Prather, who had made it clear that he considered the smaller man to be a bit of a prig. But, in Keith's view, any man who could work two spaniels simultaneously among rabbits and remain in control could be forgiven anything short of regicide.

'I've just been reading the transcript,' Keith said. 'Tell me about your tiff with Miss Spalding.'

Hugh Donald laughed. His laugh was attractive and infectious and Keith could see why he had been predisposed to like him. 'Tiff is about the right word,'

Donald said. 'In many ways, I liked the woman. She was the sturdy, mannish sort, the kind who would like horses but despise hunting. I liked to go out there early in the morning and give the dogs a workout on the rabbits or do a little decoying for pigeons. She was an early riser like myself, and she used to attach herself to me. Her sympathy was with the rabbits. She was entitled to her opinions and I told her so, but she couldn't see that that didn't entitle her to ruin my legitimate sport. On any other subject we got along all right. Sometimes I'd give up all prospect of a shot and we'd just have a walk and a talk, putting the world to rights. And she loved to watch the dogs working, provided that it wasn't on anything live. She was quite helpful about throwing dummies.

'After I failed to get my interdict – which she took as a bit of a joke – I made up my mind that there was only one thing for it. I was going to start asking around until I had permission to go onto half-a-dozen farms and could take my pick on a morning or evening. That would have spoiled her little game. But with the arrival of oil-rich sportsmen from all over the world, there's a lot of pressure on the land near Aberdeen. Up to the time of the murder, I hadn't found anywhere else. I wasn't in any hurry. With the season starting, I was going to be busy enough acting as host on the Shennilco shoot.'

Keith glanced back through the transcript. 'This business about the number. When did you insure the gun?'

'I'm afraid I forgot about it until I was filing your receipt.'

'And then you took the number off the receipt, not off the gun itself?'

Hugh Donald nodded.

'Who knew that you'd cashed that cheque, the night

33

before it all happened?'

Donald shrugged. 'The bar was fairly full.'

'You weren't manoeuvred into cashing it?'

'Lord no! That landlord doesn't like credit cards, but he often takes my cheque if I want to buy another round.'

'Could your pocket have been picked immediately afterwards?'

'I think not,' Hugh Donald said. 'The police asked the same question and so did Prather, and I've only got the one answer. I think that I remember my cheque book among the things I put into my pockets the next morning. If that's so, it would have been in my jacket pocket, locked in the car, while I was on the foreshore. There was no sign of the car being entered, not that I noticed, but a piece of wire would be all that a moderately skilful thief would have needed. I never noticed its loss until that night. And then I thought that I must have left it somewhere, until the police suddenly produced it.'

Jeremy Prather, looking altogether fresher and brighter, had arrived in the doorway a few seconds earlier but had waited for Hugh Donald to finish speaking. Now, taking the decrepit swivel chair behind the typist's desk, he spoke as if he had had a part in the whole discussion.

'Which leads one to suspect a more organised and less impromptu crime,' he said. 'If the murder and the theft of the cheque book were more or less simultaneous, we have at least two men working in concert – one committing the crime, the other following you in the hope of stealing something which would put you on the scene at the time of the murder. Right?' he asked Keith.

'That's how I see it,' Keith said.

'I'd made it no secret that I was in two minds whether to greet the opening of the wildfowling season with a visit to the foreshore,' Hugh Donald said thoughtfully. 'The geese wouldn't have been here yet, but there was always the chance of a duck. My luck was out or I might at least have had a mallard or two to back me up. Suppose I'd changed my mind and gone rabbiting instead?'

'Almost certainly there'd have been a murder and suicide,' said Keith. 'That may have been the main intention with the other plan as a back-up. Was anybody seen near the place where the body was found, between the time of the murder and the finding of the cheque book?'

'Not that I could discover,' Prather said. 'The police weren't too helpful.'

'They usually aren't, during the currency of the case,' Keith said. 'But now, their records will have been filed away as dead . . .'

'Not dead,' Prather corrected him. 'Dormant. They can re-open the case against Hugh. We can't, but they can. You see, he's been neither cleared nor convicted.'

This put into Keith's mind a complicated plan to induce a fresh prosecution by means of evidence which would prove unsound during the new trial, to be followed by the revelation of new evidence for the defence which had been cunningly concealed in the precognitions of the witnesses. But, unless Prather was remarkably open-minded about his professional responsibilities, it was a course to be pursued without the knowledge of the lawyers. He filed it away in his mind for later consideration.

'Dormant, then,' he said patiently. 'By which I mean that the investigating officers will no longer be sitting on all the evidence. I'll bet there were a thousand things found and a hundred statements taken which you never set eyes on. They'll be shelved now.'

'I could try for a court order,' Prather said.

'Bad idea,' Keith said. 'Things can vanish. D'you have a pet bobby who owes you favours?'

'I do, but he wasn't on the case.'

'Try him anyway,' Keith said.

There was a knock at the door. Molly's cousin Sheila put her head in, spotted Keith and came inside. 'Here I am at last,' she said.

Sheila McDowell was a woman nearing thirty but looking less. Unlike her cousin she was spectacular without quite being beautiful, but the plainness of her features was apt to pass unnoticed, at least until the observer had got used to the well-groomed hair of flaming red, the large, green eyes, perfect complexion, with such little makeup as it needed being applied with subtle skill, and a figure which seemed noticeably designed to be cuddled rather than admired from a distance. The three men stood up, Keith less precipitately than the others. He could sense a whole new set of vibrations in the room as he performed the introductions.

'Sorry if I've kept you waiting,' she said cheerfully. 'Molly told me what it was all about, but she said to go and see Shennilco before coming here. And – what do you think? – I start with them as soon as you've finished with me! So . . . where do I work and what do you want me to do?'

'You can take over this room and we'll go into my private den,' Prather said. 'I have a temp comes in occasionally to deal with my typing, but I can just as easily send it round to her.' He moved away from the desk chair.

'Your first job's to phone Spain,' Keith said. 'Molly says you speak good Spanish.'

'I don't know about good, just enough to get by on holiday. But I'll try.'

'That's all we can ask.' Keith bent over the desk and

started scribbling. 'The man you want is a Señor Tomelloso. I think the first name was Esteban. He was with Armas Alicante until they were taken over and I think he stayed with the new parent firm, Garcia Y Thomaso. If you can reach him, or anyone else who worked with Alicante, these are the questions.'

Sheila looked them over. 'Golly!' she said. 'Do we have a Spanish dictionary?'

'Go out and buy one,' Prather said.

FOUR

Jeremy Prather's personal den turned out to be even less inspiring than his outer office. In addition to similarly dilapidated furniture and some untidy stacks of papers, files and books, it also housed what Keith guessed to be the overflow from his flat of a collection of ill-assorted curios ranging from stuffed animal heads to a samurai sword. But at least it contained the more comfortable chairs.

'Mr Donald—' Keith began.

'Let's keep it informal,' Prather said. 'Keith, Hugh and Jeremy, all right?'

Keith cared very little who called who what, but Hugh Donald's agreement was unenthusiastic. Solicitor and client might have respected each other's professional abilities but there was no rapport at a personal level. Which, Keith thought, might explain a certain half-heartedness in the preparation of the defence.

'Hugh, then,' he said. 'We've agreed that this crime was pre-planned. It may be a mistake to think about motives too early, but let's risk wasting a little time. On the face of it, it looks as if the objective was to dispose of Miss Spalding, for one of perhaps a dozen reasons. But before we concentrate on her there's the alternative that the intention was to get you out of the way.

'I don't like that idea, but—'

'Why not?' Jeremy asked.

'Because there was no way that they could have been

38

sure that Hugh wouldn't meet friends on the foreshore or exchange waves with the Lord Provost or break down and have to phone for a tow. And if he'd had an alibi it would have negated the whole plan. But there may be some reason why I'm wrong. It's even possible that somebody said to himself, "I need this woman out of the way, and I have access to a gun which is still registered in the name of a man who's on bad terms with her. And, what's more, I'd be happy if Hugh Donald were removed at the same stroke. So that's the way we'll do it." You follow me?'

His listeners nodded.

'So,' Keith said, 'you must ask yourself whether you can think of anybody who would profit from your going, somebody who also had a connection with Miss Spalding. Your depute, for instance. Will he inherit your job?'

'I doubt it,' Hugh said.

'Has he been dipping his fingers in the till while you've been inside?'

'That's the next thing I was intending to find out,' Hugh said grimly.

'Think it over and make a list of people who might want you out of the way. Add any links that you know of with Miss Spalding. And we may be looking for a connection with somebody taller and thinner than you are, or possibly taller and left-handed.

'And now,' Keith went on, 'let's see what leads we can follow up. I may be covering ground you've already been over, Jeremy. If so, tell me how far you got. All right?'

'We'll be going up a hundred dead ends,' Jeremy said. 'But I suppose it's necessary.'

'It is.' Keith was in no mood to waste time in saving the solicitor's face. 'Let's start with the gun. Hugh, I know that it was five years ago, but the occasion of

39

buying a new gun tends to stick in the memory. Tell me all you can remember about the purchase. Why did you come to my shop instead of to somebody local?'

'I had to come to Newton Lauder on business,' Hugh said. 'One of our consultants was on a shooting holiday there and I needed his signature on a contract.'

'Tell me about him.'

Hugh pulled a bunch of small diaries out of his pocket, selected one and thumbed through it. 'His name seems to have been Naulty. Initial M. He was with a firm which got swallowed up shortly afterwards so I haven't seen him for years. I couldn't even tell you what he looked like.'

'Was he taller and thinner than yourself?'

'Everybody's taller and thinner than I am,' Hugh pointed out. 'I was new to my present job, and it had just been made clear to me that, as the only shooting man among the upper executives, I was to play host on the firm's shoot. I'd been using a battered old pump-gun, which was hardly suitable for formal days at driven game. I seem to remember lunching with Naulty at a big hotel in the square, and by way of lunch-time chat I mentioned my need of a new gun. He said that he'd been dealing with you for years.'

'There was a Naulty,' Keith said, remembering. 'I think he went abroad.'

'Oh? Well, after lunch we walked over to your shop and a fair-haired young woman showed us your stock of guns. To be honest,' Hugh added, 'I remember her rather better than I do anything else.'

Keith nodded. Janet, his partner's wife, tended to have that effect on men. 'Go on,' he said.

'Naulty recommended the Armas Alicante sidelock as the best value for money in the shop.'

'He could have been right. Did he say that he had one of them himself?'

40

'Not that I remember. But it felt good and it was smart enough not to disgrace me on a formal day. You came in about then, and you suggested that I might be better with the stock a quarter of an inch shorter. As it turned out, you were right and I had it done a few months later. So I bought it, and a new bag to go with it and some cartridges.'

'You didn't tell me about Naulty,' Jeremy said.

'I didn't have my diaries with me.'

'We'll move on,' Keith said firmly. He had no objection to being well paid to listen to a client and his solicitor bickering, but he had no intention of allowing them to prolong his stay in Aberdeen. 'Accidentally or on purpose, a similar gun was swapped for your own. It must have happened very soon after you bought it. It's very easy to pick up the wrong gun at a shoot, for instance, but if you've already been using it for a time the weight and balance feel wrong immediately even if the guns look similar. So tell us about the next few days. When you got home, did you take the new gun out and gloat over it?'

'Nothing like that. I was too damn busy,' Hugh said. 'I found time to leave my old gun with a gunsmith to sell for me, but the new gun stayed in its bag in the boot of my car until my first time on the Shennilco shoot, a few days later.'

Keith disapproved strongly of guns being left in bags or in car boots, but he could read a lecture another time. 'Could a substitution have happened that day, at your first Shennilco shoot?' he asked.

'Very easily,' Hugh said. 'I was harassed to hell and back. The day was a disaster, that much I do remember. It was blowing a gale and the birds went everywhere except over the guns. There was an old keeper – he retired soon afterwards and he's died since – who had always been left to do everything his own way, and he

41

resented my very existence. So he insisted on being told what to do every inch of the way, and being young and ignorant I made every mistake in the book. I think the keeper was the only person who enjoyed himself.'

'So if one of the guests had found that he'd come away with the wrong gun, and thought to himself, "It's the same model as mine and in just as good condition, so why should I bother?", you'd never have noticed?'

'I don't think I would. In fact, I have a dim recollection of cleaning the gun for the first time that evening and being surprised that the grain of the stock seemed not to be as I'd remembered it and that there were a couple of slight scratches which I couldn't remember putting there.'

'Who were the guests that day?' Keith asked.

Hugh sighed. 'We just don't know,' he said. 'The old keeper kept the shoot records and he took them with him. They can't be found. Hundreds of business contacts have been invited since, but from among all the faces competing in my memory I can't single out the ones who were there that day. The only person I remember for sure is Naulty. We were going to be one man short so I invited him and he jumped at it.'

The appearance of Molly's cousin in the doorway cut short a lengthy discussion of Mr Naulty. 'I have Señor Tomelloso on the line,' she said. 'He says that only one series of numbers was allocated to guns in the style of their export sidelock, whatever that is, and the numbers started from nought-nought-nought-one. And he wants to know when his ol' frien' Keats is coming back to drink more brandy with him.'

'Thank him very much for the help,' Keith said, 'and tell him never. The last time nearly killed me.' For a moment, the hot sun and dusty smells seemed to pervade the chilly office. 'Then come back. There are some more calls.'

'Yes Mr Calder, sir,' she said.

'I take it that the four-figure start precludes the numbers having been tampered with?' Jeremy said.

'That's why I had Sheila ask the question. It would have been comparatively easy to add a digit before or after a three-figure number.' Keith looked up as Sheila appeared again. 'Phone Newton Lauder,' he said. 'Start with my partner; he'll tell you what other numbers to call. We want news of a Mr M Naulty. He used to be a client at the shop. He had at least one shooting holiday in the area about five years ago, so he was either a guest of one of the shoot owners or staying at the Inverburn Hotel. What did he look like? Was he left-handed? What gun did he use? Did he ever buy an Armas Alicante sidelock off us? And whatever happened to him? That and any other gossip you can dig up. Then get onto one of the bigger Scottish newspapers and find out whether any gunshops in Scotland have burned during the last few months, say from the beginning of August, other than the one we know about in Aberdeen.'

'To hear is to obey,' she said as she departed.

Keith frowned at Hugh Donald. 'You're sure you want to have so much bright girlhood around Shennilco?' he asked.

'I'm sure,' Hugh said, half smiling. 'Even if secretaries weren't at a premium, the place could do with brightening.' He stopped smiling suddenly. 'Why another gunshop?'

'It's a long shot. If – and it's a big if – somebody burned one shop to destroy your chance of proving that you've been using a different gun for years, he might also have wanted to erase any record that he'd been the original purchaser of the gun which was in your hands all that time, or that he'd had your gun in his possession long enough to have had it altered to fit him.'

'I thought that would be it,' Hugh said.

'If there's no record of another gunshop fire,' Keith said, 'Sheila's going to have to phone every gunshop in Britain and ask them to look back five years in their records. And half of them,' he added sadly, 'will say they've looked without bothering to do it and most of the others will avoid the labour by saying that the information's confidential. There's been a lot of pressure from the police to get shotguns registered like firearms, and there'd be a lot less resistance if they didn't go out of their way to make life difficult and expensive for the firearm's owner. That's another matter. But if the police had a computerised register of shotgun ownership, this sort of quest would be easier and fewer gunshops would get burned. There was an attempt on my shop once, for much the same reason.'

Jeremy Prather had been thinking. The act, so early and after a hard night, seemed to pain him. He lit another cigarette and coughed. 'If two thousand five hundred and something guns were made, and presumably more after that one, and most of them were exported to this country, we're going to get a hell of a list of purchasers. And, as you said, many of them will have changed hands without any record.'

'True,' Keith said. 'But when I alter a gun's dimensions I make a note of them. Then the customer can order similar work on another gun over the phone and be sure that it'll fit him.'

Sheila came to the door again. 'I tried the newspapers first,' she said. 'According to *The Scotsman*, the only other fire since August happened last night. A big gunshop in Glasgow. It's still burning. Arson seems to be suspected.'

'So much for that lead,' Keith said. 'Somebody may be thinking one jump ahead of us. Thank you, Sheila. And *hasta luego*,' he added when she seemed inclined to linger.

'Are my dogs behaving?' Hugh asked her.

'Good as gold.'

'Dogs?' Jeremy said sharply. 'I won't have dogs in here, rampaging all over the place.'

'If they were rampaging all over the place, you'd have known they were here before now,' Hugh pointed out. Jeremy grunted and fell silent.

Keith waited until Sheila had, with ostentatious gentleness, closed the connecting door. 'I have friends in Glasgow, reporters and in the police, so I'll stay in touch with that one. There may be no connection, but we may learn something.

'Let's move on. What do we know about Miss Spalding?'

Jeremy Prather produced another slim file. 'Little more than you'll have seen in the transcript,' he said. 'Mostly such gossip as I could pick up.'

Keith skimmed through the few pages and found a photograph. Mary Spalding had been handsome in a square, masculine way. Keith judged that she had had charm without sex-appeal. 'According to these notes,' he said, 'her relationships with men were platonic. Golf, the occasional meal, not even a little footsie under the table.'

'That was the word,' Jeremy said.

'Any suggestion of a lesbian relationship?'

'It was mentioned. It could even be true – how on earth do you prove or disprove a thing like that? But I took it for the reaction of a man who'd made a pass and been turned down.'

'You could be right. What do we know about the woman she shared the house with?'

Jeremy handed over another file.

Keith stayed with Miss Spalding for the moment. 'There's very little here about her work,' he said.

'It's all I could get. Her firm refused to discuss her

45

work at all. Grounds of confidentiality.'

'I wonder. Accountants are the people most likely to know too much. Jeremy, that's your next task.'

'I've already done all I can,' Jeremy protested. 'I hit a brick wall.'

Keith looked across the stacked desk. 'Nonsense,' he said. 'If you want the dirt, don't ask the firm. Ask their biggest rivals. You're a lawyer, you must have contacts with accountants.'

'Well, yes.'

'Use them.'

The file on Miss Spalding's friend contained only one typed sheet and a blurred, amateurish photograph. Jenny Carlogie was thin, with fair, curly hair and an anxious expression. She cycled regularly to her work as receptionist and assistant manageress in a country hotel and spent her leisure hours at home. No relationships with men, platonic or otherwise, were known. She was efficient at her work, but, although her colleagues liked her, none had claimed her as a friend.

'Very sparse,' Keith said.

'It's all there was,' Jeremy said defensively. 'I went to see her but she clammed up on me.'

'I'll have a go at her later,' Keith said. 'I noticed that her only evidence was that Miss Spalding had gone out early but as usual.'

'There wasn't much more for her to say except that her friend had gone out to harass the defendant. I mean Hugh. That would have been hearsay and not best evidence, and it was already implicit.'

'You're guessing again. I bet her statement to the police and the precognition which she originally gave the prosecution lawyers say a whole lot more. I'd like to see them. In fact, I want to see all the precognitions and all the material gathered by the police. Photographs especially. Then I'll spend an hour or two in your outer

46

office digesting them and helping out on the telephone.'

Jeremy pushed a stack of files to the front of the desk. 'Precognitions,' he said. 'But only the ones prepared for the trial; they exclude any material not used in court.'

'In other words,' Keith said, 'they leave out anything which might possibly be of use to the defence?'

'You're getting there. In the envelope, you'll find the photographs which were in evidence. Use this room. I'll see if I can get access to the rest of the police material. But I'm not hopeful.'

'It's like running in treacle,' Keith complained.

The solicitor nodded patiently. 'Now you're getting an idea what I've been up against. And I'll talk to some accountants. Between times, I'll try to solve some of the problems of my own clients.'

'You do that,' Keith said. He turned to Hugh Donald. 'Could you come back for me after lunch?' he asked. 'I'd like to be taken out and shown the ground, and to pay a call on Miss Carlogie'.

FIVE

Suspecting – rightly, as he later learned – that the press release from Shennilco would have brought reporters to the hotel, Keith snatched a quick lunch in a small restaurant. Around him were the diverse accents of the oil world, Scots, English, Texan, Dutch, Norwegian and others which he could not identify. He ignored them, re-examining instead the notes which Sheila had typed up for him from Jeremy's tape-recorder. A quick skim through the precognitions seemed to produce remarkably little information of forseeable usefulness. He took out the photographs, holding them where the other lunchers could not see them. Out of context, they meant very little.

He was back in Jeremy's office by two. Sheila was out for her own lunch but had left him a note. A guarded message relayed from the shop confirmed that Molly and Deborah had arrived safely. And if M Naulty had owned an Armas Alicante sidelock, he had neither bought it from nor had it serviced by the firm. He was remembered, but the general opinion was that his build had been average. Wallace, Keith's partner, had added an anxious message about outstanding gun repairs. Keith scribbled a frivolous reply for Sheila to relay.

Hugh Donald arrived a few minutes later, in a large, new estate car. The two spaniels, Keith noted with approval, were comfortably bedded in the tail.

'I brought a pair of boots for you,' Hugh said. 'I hope

48

you can get into them.'

'I have very small feet for my size,' Keith said with dignity.

He knew the geography and had expected to leave Aberdeen by way of Bucksburn and over the Tyre-bagger. But that route, Hugh explained, was nowadays clogged with traffic to and from Dyce Airport at all major and minor rush hours. They went out by Skene and cut over a minor road, where only the passing of other traffic had made an impression on the snow. Keith began to see the bulk of Bennachie dominating the further skyline, white against a sky which was darkening again.

Hugh coaxed the big car over slippery roads with practised skill. They were still in the flat valley of Donside when he brought the car to a halt in the mouth of a farm track. A permanent fence a few yards from the mouth suggested that the track was no longer used by farm machinery. 'From here,' Hugh said, 'we walk.'

'Don't rush me.' Keith looked around. The nearest house was several hundred yards away. 'Is that where the car was seen from? Nobody could recognise an individual from there. And dogs, or the lack of them, would be screened by the hedge. Where was the cyclist when he saw the figure which he thought was you?'

'About here, I think.'

'Can you see Miss Spalding's bungalow from here?'

'If you crane your neck. It's further up the slope and slightly behind us. To the left of that tract of gorse and below the pimple on the skyline.'

Keith craned his neck. The bungalow seemed to be the only other dwelling within a mile. It had a clear view of their parking place. 'Was it the sight of your car that brought her down?' he asked.

'I doubt it. I sometimes tried parking where it was hidden from the bungalow, but she turned up all the same. I think she always took her morning leg stretch in this direction.'

'Let's do the same,' Keith said.

The boots, without the customary extra pair of socks, were no more than slightly snug. They crossed the fence. The two spaniels waited until told and then took it in a leap. At a flick of their master's finger they were off, tearing in wide circles and sampling the snowy ground, ecstatic after months in kennels. But soon they sobered and fell back into working pattern, quartering the ground, half a gunshot ahead of the two men. Their breaths smoked in the cold air.

Hugh Donald set a pace which Keith had to step out to match. They were following field boundaries. Under the snow, Keith could not tell pasture from winter barley; but occasionally he could make out the texture of ploughed land. Some woodpigeon went up from the remains of a cattle-crop and then a flock of grey geese – pinkfooted, Keith knew from the 'wink-wink' call.

They came to broken ground between dry-stone walls, where no farmer had found it worth his while to plough. It was a place where boulders and gorse showed above the snow, and Keith could see the tracks and droppings of many rabbits.

'This is the place,' Hugh said.

Keith produced the envelope of photographs and oriented himself. 'She seems to have been found about where you're standing,' he said. It seemed to be an offence against Miss Spalding's right to dignity in death that he should be studying a photograph, in full colour, of her last, ungainly sprawl. 'Stay there and mark the place. Unless you'd care to lie down and simulate the body?'

Hugh Donald preferred to remain on his feet.

A few yards away stood a clump of elders. Keith could see the ground and the sky through them but in

50

September, as the photographs showed, they would have provided perfect cover for an assassin lying in wait. Faint tracks, carefully recorded among the photographs, suggested that this was what had happened.

Keith spent several minutes wandering round with the photographs, looking this way and that until he had identified the place where the rabbit had been found, against a dry-stone wall and some thirty yards from where the body had lain. He squatted down and studied the rough granite stones carefully and then rose again. His knees annoyed him by creaking, a sign of the passing years. 'What happened to the rabbit?' he asked. 'Did they keep it?'

'They had it in cold store somewhere,' Hugh said. 'They asked me whether I wanted it, when they turned me loose. I said that it wasn't mine, never had been, and they could keep it.'

'Well, change your mind quickly,' Keith said. 'We want it. That's a VIB.'

'Huh?'

'Very Important Bunny.' Keith turned and leaned against the wall. 'Look at it this way. The presence of that rabbit added a very strong presumption that you, the one man who shot rabbits around here, were there that morning. A visiting killer wouldn't be expected to go out after rabbits; and the sound of a shot would draw Miss Spalding here with all her prejudices rising like hackles. I don't believe that the killer was lucky enough to get the chance of a rabbit and took it just to make the story look better.

'You can still see the marks of the pellets on the stones. The rabbit received a dose of shot against this wall where it was found. So he didn't bring it here with shot already in it. You follow me?'

Hugh Donald nodded doubtfully.

'My guess would be that the killer arrived here, put

51

the rabbit against the wall and waited for Miss Spalding to arrive. He killed her and put his second shot into the rabbit and then departed.

'The pathologist doesn't seem to have done a post mortem examination of poor bunny, just pulled out a few pellets to make sure that they matched the ones in the body.'

Hugh was catching up. 'He'd have noticed that the pellet wounds hadn't bled,' he said.

'Not through fur. But the killer couldn't risk two different lots of shot in the rabbit. I'd guess that he brought a dead but unmarked rabbit with him. And how do you get one of those in late August?'

'From the butcher or game dealer.'

'Probably. But the point is, how was it killed? Wrong time of year for satisfactory ferreting. If it has a broken neck or the mark of a wire snare, we've learned something. I have an idea about that. We're lucky that the police photographer seems to have been an enthusiast – very good photographs, and in colour. We'd better have that rabbit collected before some daft bobby eats the evidence. If he didn't have it for lunch today.'

Keith looked down at the photographs again. Only one showed even part of an identifiable boot print, in softer ground near what Keith took to be the rising of a small spring. He asked Hugh Donald, 'Did the police ever match this to your boots?'

'No. But, as they pointed out more than once, I have several pairs of Royal Hunters and I could have had more. My counsel was going to argue that I could have made the track days before, if I made it at all.'

'It looks pretty fresh in the photograph,' Keith said. 'But a jury might not have known the difference. What other footprints were found?'

Hugh shrugged. 'The farmer and one of his sons walked up this way and found the body,' he said. 'And it's a common enough route for strollers. If they found more than you see there, they never told me. Or the court.'

'These are only the photographs prepared for the trial,' Keith said thoughtfully. 'I bet they took a thousand photographs of other tracks, if we can only get our hands on them.'

'But if the murderer wore Hunters—' Hugh began.

'I'm thinking of later. While your lady friend was being killed, it would seem that somebody else was stealing your cheque book from your car. So one of them had to make another visit here, to drop it where it would do you most harm, and preferably without being seen. Especially not being seen from where we parked the car. Which way would he have come?'

Hugh led him back and across their original route. Beyond another dry-stone wall was the head of a gulley. 'That runs most of the way to the Don,' he said.

There seemed to be a burn, now frozen, following the bottom of the small valley. 'It must've been damp down there,' Keith said. 'I wish to God I could have seen around at the time, not months later and under snow. Well, that's the way it crumbles. We'll just have to hope that Jeremy can get his hands on the rest of the photographs, and that the police were conscientious enough to make a record so far from the body.'

'We'll be lucky,' Hugh said bitterly.

'Listen, Sunshine,' Keith said. 'I don't want to depress you but there's something you ought to know. We've *got* to be lucky. If we aren't, you're going to carry the taint of murder for the rest of your days. We don't have the resources of the police, they're not going to offer us any help and if we get access to the statements they took it'll be by way of the back door and Jeremy's pal. The scent's cold. The police depend on luck to help solve most of their cases. We've got nothing else going for us at all. But don't let me worry you. Let's go and see Miss Carlogie. Tea and scones wouldn't come amiss after this walk in the cold.'

They returned, in depressed silence, to the car. Hugh raised his eyebrows. 'Let's try the hotel first,' Keith said.

It was a bad guess. When they found Miss Carlogie's place of employment, a former private mansion now functioning as an hotel and catering mainly for shooting and fishing guests, an elderly man in a dark suit which could have passed for a porter's uniform was on the desk. It was Miss Carlogie's afternoon off, he said. She would be on duty again at six. Keith phoned a message to Sheila for Jeremy about the rabbit and they faced the cold again.

'Head for the bungalow,' Keith said. And as they turned out of the hotel drive, 'Is this the road she'd cycle on to work?'

'I expect so.'

'Do we pass near the bottom of that gulley?'

'Quite near,' Hugh said.

'Let's look at the nearest parking place to it.'

Hugh pointed to the bottom of the gulley, although the contours were indiscernible under the virgin snow and only the field boundaries gave any sense of shape. He drove on a few yards. The road had been routed to bypass a huge sycamore tree on one side and the fence detoured around the tree on the other, leaving a widened verge on which Hugh parked. Keith twisted his head round to take another good look. But even the wire strands of the fence were topped with snow.

'If we get a thaw,' he said, 'I'll come back with my brother-in-law. But even then I wouldn't be hopeful after such a time. Drive on. You'd better park where she can't see your face until I find out whether she has her knife into you.'

Hugh drove on, turned into a side road and parked in line with the gable of the cottage. Keith, who had changed back into shoes, picked his way carefully to the front door. He noticed cycle tracks and a few ladylike footprints, but most of his mind was taken up with the problem of how to make the best impression on a possible lesbian. Manly charm? Mildly effeminate? Little boy lost? He decided, as he rang the bell, to smile and improvise.

Jenny Carlogie answered the chimes and blinked at him. She was smaller than he had expected from the photograph, just as thin but, under concealing woollies, bustier. The anxious expression was emphasised by nervous hand movements.

He had expected a sexless woman, one of the near neuters who seek only the companionship of their own kind, but he was surprised to detect an extreme of femininity. It was not just in the delicate features and the articulation of her small bones and the fact that she was fluffy of hair and clothing. Something about her pleaded to be protected and cosseted. In addition, Keith could sense that she responded instantly to him. In his youth Keith had been handsome in a dark and gypsyish way and middle age had not been unkind to him. He saw her recognise his maleness. Simultaneously, they smiled. Her smile was shy and yet it was unreserved. He decided that Jeremy Prather would have to learn to smile at witnesses.

'I'm sorry to trouble you at home,' Keith said. 'I called at the hotel. It's about the recent trial. After a verdict of not proven some further investigation is necessary.'

'But you're not police, are you?'

Keith had hoped to imply that he was, but he switched tactics instantly. 'Shennilco have engaged me to do a full and impartial investigation,' he said.

'Naturally, they hope that the results will clear their employee, but . . .'

'You'd better come in,' she said. She craned her neck towards the car.

'Just my driver,' Keith said. 'He'll do fine where he is.'

She took him into a sitting room, severely decorated but embellished with some discordant fripperies. As they sat down, Keith could feel the outline of a modern, Swedish chair through the chintz cover. There were several uninformative photographs of the late Mary Mae Spalding. The red eye of a modern burglar alarm winked at him.

'You must be Mr Calder,' Miss Carlogie said. 'It came over on the news, that Shennilco had asked you to investigate. I don't suppose I can help, but I will if I can.'

Even without Jeremy Prather's report, Keith would have expected hostility rather than such co-operation from someone who might well think that Hugh Donald had killed her friend. He had to think quickly to find an innocuous first question. 'Tell me about your friend, as a person,' he said.

Her eyes brimmed immediately. 'She was a really nice person. She could never do enough for me. I . . . . I don't know what else I can say.'

It was hardly an unbiased testimonial, Keith thought, but it had broken the ice. 'Do you know anything about her work?' he asked.

'Very little. I know she was very good at it. They called her the Computer Queen. She got her firm to put everything onto computer and she oversaw the running of it, but she also did the accounts for some quite big firms herself. She even had her own computer here and she used to bring work home to do on it. She was terribly conscientious.'

56

Keith began to feel that Miss Carlogie was not only fluffy of hair and jumper but of mind as well. This was no great surprise, despite her job. In his experience simple-minded people, well instructed, often grasped the logic and method of their work when, outside of it, they hardly had the sense to scratch where it itched. Her comments on her dearest friend were as superficial as a topping of whipped cream. He struggled on.

'Do you know who was her next of kin?' he asked.

'A cousin. In Canada, I think.'

'And he or she inherits any money that Miss Spalding left?'

'Oh no,' Miss Carlogie said. 'She left it all to me. What there is of it.'

There was a false note in her voice. Keith pricked up his mental ears. For the first time he felt that he was approaching something new. 'Was she not the saving sort?' he asked carefully.

'We weren't very extravagant,' she said. 'Of course, I get her half of the house. And she had a few hundred pounds in the bank. That was all.'

'It surprised you?'

'Well, it did. I knew that she had investments and things, because we were talking about retiring and going away. Somewhere warm and peaceful. So there must be more somewhere. I don't mind too much,' she added earnestly, 'because I wouldn't want to go away on my own. But it does seem a pity.'

Keith's preference usually ran to self-reliant women, but Miss Carlogie was beginning to have for him some of the appeal of a shy labrador puppy. 'Could she have had a box in a safe-deposit?' he asked.

'If she had, the police couldn't find it.'

'You asked them to help?'

'They asked me if she'd had a safe-deposit box and I said that I didn't think so. Later on, they told me that

57

they couldn't find such a thing.'

There was something there, but Keith pushed it aside for the moment. 'I suppose you've looked among her papers?'

She hesitated. The nervous movements became more pronounced. 'I couldn't,' she said at last. 'The house was broken into, just a day or two after she was killed. Our jewels went, such as they were, and all the silver. But they also took all her papers, every scrap. And even her gramophone records.'

'You called the police?'

'Yes, of course.'

'And didn't they connect it with the fact that she'd just been killed?'

'They said that there might be a connection. But it turned out that the man they arrested for the murder was making a statement at about the time of the burglary, so they said that it must just have been a coincidence, or that the news of Mary's death might have called somebody's attention to a lonely house which would probably be empty all day. The police kept an eye on the house for a few days, and when they stopped somebody came back. But by then the police had recommended a man who does burglar alarms, and I'd had the house protected. It cost me most of my savings, but that's a small price for feeling safe, don't you think? It's linked right to the police station, you know. They don't usually like having it that way, but because I'm a woman living on my own, and a bit nervous, they let me have it. So the local police got here before he could take anything else,' she finished breathlessly.   .

'But you never told the police that you thought a lot of her money was missing?'

'No. But I think they knew. A different man, a senior policeman, asked me a lot of questions which I couldn't

58

have answered if I'd wanted to.'

There was the clue again. She was almost pushing the answers at him, consciously or not. He decided to come at it again from another angle. 'You're being wonderfully helpful,' he said. 'I can't thank you enough.'

She turned pink. 'It's the least I can do,' she said.

'You think that Hugh Donald was innocent, don't you?' Keith said.

'I thought that he might be.'

'Was it something that happened just before Miss Spalding was killed?'

'Not exactly.' She stopped and stared out of the window. Snow was falling again. The room had become dark. She got up and switched on the lights before deciding to go on. 'But she wasn't her usual self. It was if she was afraid of something. She told me not to open the door to strange men, not even to say anything to them through the letter box. She went on and on about it, and I realised afterwards that she'd let me know, without saying it directly, that I wasn't to say anything to the police if they came.'

'I understand,' Keith said. 'So, after she was killed and her money seemed to have disappeared, you felt that least said, soonest mended. And that included the defence solicitor.'

She looked happier. 'That's it exactly.' A clock chimed somewhere in the house. 'I'll have to go soon,' she said.

Keith wanted time to think before he pushed her any further. He changed ground. 'What happened on the morning she died?' he asked. 'Did you go to your work?'

'I was late. Mary usually came back and left again in her Mini before I biked off, because she had further to go. But that morning she didn't come back. And I was worried, because of what she'd said. So I waited a bit and then I phoned the farmer and he said he'd keep an eye out for her. And then the hotel phoned, to find out if I was ill or something, and I said no, just a domestic crisis and I was coming right away.'

'I know that it's a journey you do every day,' Keith said, 'but, if you can remember that morning in particular, did you see a car parked where the big sycamore is, about a mile from here?'

'I remember very well,' she said. 'You see, I was worried about Mary, so I was watching the farmland as I went, instead of riding along in a dream as I usually do. And yes, there was a car parked where you said. At first I thought that it was Mr Donald's car, the one which he usually parked just down the hill from here, but it didn't look quite the same.'

'Was anybody in or near it?' Keith asked.

'No. But I saw a man coming down that little valley. I couldn't tell you what he looked like, because as soon as he saw me glance up he stepped behind a bush. Frankly, I thought that he'd gone there to have a widdle,' Miss Carlogie said delicately.

'Was that in the precognition which you gave to the Fiscal's office? And the burglary?'

'Both of them,' she said. 'But they had me sign a shorter copy before the trial.'

'What else did they leave out?' Keith asked quickly.

'Nothing much that I can think of. Except for the phone call. I'll tell you about it. Just a few days before she . . . died . . . there was a phone call. I answered it and it was a man's voice asking for Mary. She was in and she took it over. I don't know what was said but it seemed to upset her. That was when she started warning me not to talk to anybody, but I didn't say anything about that in my statement.'

'You didn't hear her end of the conversation?'

'She didn't say much, just listened. If it helps, the

60

man's voice sounded just a bit deeper than yours, but there was no accent that I noticed.'

'Could it have been Hugh Donald's voice?'

'I told them I was sure that it wasn't. He phoned up once, before he took Mary to court. His voice was higher, and over the phone there was a north-of-England accent which you don't notice otherwise. And now, I really must be going in a minute. I'm on duty tonight. Tomorrow I'm working all day and off in the evening,' she added, as if this was a matter which could not possibly be of interest.

'I'll remember,' Keith said.

While they talked, she had unconsciously been adjusting her posture to be a mirror image of his own, and yet modifying it so that the outline of breast or thigh was shown to advantage. And Keith, who was sensitive to such things, detected signs of arousal, even, as they got up to shake hands, the smell of it beyond her faint perfume. He thought that somebody as shy as Jenny Carlogie, and with as much repressed sexuality, would be a pushover for any seducer, male or female.

SIX

Miss Carlogie was pleased to accept a lift to her work, with her bicycle stowed beside the dogs and hanging half over the back seat. She set the alarms carefully before leaving home. The hotel, she explained, could usually find her a bed if the snow became too bad, but she was well used to the ride in all conditions. Her manner towards Hugh Donald was friendly, curious and slightly flirtatious.

They dropped her at the hotel and turned back for Aberdeen. Hugh opted for the cross-country road again and nursed the car carefully over the new carpet of snow.

'At least we can be sure nobody's following us around,' Keith said.

Hugh cocked an eye at him. 'You're expecting something like that?'

'Not necessarily. But it's always possible when someone's got something to hide and may be getting uptight about it. Lock your doors and keep looking over your shoulder until this is all over.'

'What a way to live!' Hugh said. 'All I want now is get back to a normal life. Did you get anything out of the old biddy?'

'That's no way to speak of a charming lady,' Keith said. (Hugh gave a snort.) 'Yes, I got plenty. She may yet turn out to be a key witness on your side. But I don't have it in context yet. Her late chum was up to something dodgy but the money's missing and her papers were stolen. I think I'll have to go back again. How about yourself? Were any dark deeds perpetrated during your absence from work?'

'I don't know yet. I have my suspicions. I'll go back to the office tonight and do a check, without anyone looking over my shoulder.'

'Join me for dinner first?'

'Not this time,' Hugh said, 'if you don't mind. I'll take a sandwich into the office and get on.'

'Fair enough. You can drop me in Chapel Street. I want to put some more notes on tape and phone Glasgow again.'

Keith fell into silent thought for a few miles. They rejoined the Skene road. Warm tyres had cleared the tarmac and Hugh made better time.

'There's one thing Shennilco could help with,' Keith said suddenly. 'We must, simply must, try to trace that other gun. It may have been bought and altered in the shop which was burned last night, but I doubt it. The place is more of a retail outlet. They'd accept a gun for alteration but they'd farm the work out. Somewhere, there may be a gunsmith who did the alteration and has the measurements on record. The police could find out. We don't have their resources. But Shennilco must have resources to match.'

'Easily,' Hugh said.

'I couldn't see Sheila phoning round every gunshop in the country and listing the details of several thousand guns,' Keith said. 'Do you think Shennilco could put several people onto it, and allocate a separate number for calls back?'

'I wouldn't expect any problem if the office is quiet.'

'Or should I go through Jeremy?'

'You can go through him with a load of shot for all I care,' Hugh said. 'He's a slob. The Old Man thinks the

63

sun shines out of his arse, so we're stuck with him. But I'll fix what you want. We've got an admin. officer who thrives on that sort of thing.'

'They'll have to be persistent,' Keith said. 'Most shops won't want to be bothered. Have them do it in Prather's name, and mention mine. Drive gently and I'll jot down the questions to be asked.'

'They'll be bothered,' Hugh said. 'At least, they will if they want to pick up a cash reward for information. The Old Man's got his teeth into this one.'

'Fine,' Keith said. He finished jotting. 'Did you manage to think of anybody who might want you out of the way?'

'I didn't tackle that myself,' Hugh said. 'It's not human nature to think of yourself as a universal target. The Old Man's PA and his secretary got together on it, consulting other departments where necessary. Last I heard they were nearing two hundred names and still going strong.'

'You must fairly go around stamping on people's pet corns,' Keith said.

'Not as often as that. But if you add up the suppliers whom I've black-listed for poor service or late delivery, the people who don't get orders any more because they've tried to bribe me or because I'm strict about like-for-like tendering, a few members of staff who might expect promotion if I was gone and some who got passed over or fired because I couldn't trust them, the list does rather tend to go on and on.'

Keith thought about it. The list of people who might want him out of circulation could be counted on the fingers of one foot. At least, he hoped so.

Keith stood in Chapel Street and watched the car drive away. There were no evident watchers but a great many doors and windows.

64

While he looked, he made up his mind what to do if somebody jumped him. He had been a notable brawler in his younger and wilder days, but those days were behind him and he had had to learn that the first seconds of an attack were no time to spend trying to remember the techniques of yesteryear.

There was nobody in the hallway, nobody on the stair and when he locked himself into Jeremy Prather's office it was deserted. There was no sound from upstairs and there had been no light in the flat. Jeremy Prather, presumably, was out on the town again.

He settled in the typist's chair and dialled his first call to Glasgow. While he waited for a connection he skimmed through the notes which Sheila had left for him. There was nothing which could not wait until morning.

The newspaper's telephone was answered. Keith's friendly reporter was standing by, but the evening had become quiet and he had adjourned to a nearby pub. The newspaper's telephonist gave him the number. A barman with a Glasgow accent so thick as to be almost unintelligible took the call. The reporter came to the phone. He sounded well lubricated but businesslike.

'I'm glad you called,' he said.

'Have you any news for me?' Keith asked.

'Possibly. Mr Calder, what's this on the wire about you being hired to investigate a murder in Aberdeen?'

'I haven't seen the Shennilco handout,' Keith said, 'but you can take it as factual.'

'Add something. Give us a quote. Any link with the fire you were asking about?'

Keith thought quickly. 'If I give you an extra quote, will you sit tight on my interest in the fire until I tell you? Then I'll give you a story and a half.'

'It's a deal.'

'All I can add at the moment is that I'm trying to trace

some men who seem to have dropped out of sight or gone abroad but who may be back in Scotland. There may or may not be some connection.' Keith gave a list of three fictitious names and added M Naulty to the end of it.

'What's the connection?'

'One of them may once have owned the shotgun which was substituted for Hugh Donald's gun. Now, what do you have for me?'

'Hold on.' Keith could hear the sound of rustling paper at the other end above a rumble of male voices and the clink of glasses. It sounded like a good party and he wished that he could join in. 'Mr Calder, could you suggest why there should be a substitution of guns, instead of simply stealing Mr Donald's gun to do the job?'

Keith sighed. 'Because the best time for the crime coincided with a time when he would be out with his gun. The intention was to frame Hugh Donald. That wouldn't work if he'd already reported the theft of his gun.'

'But—'

'That's the lot,' Keith said firmly, 'and you could have worked that much out for yourself. If you want to be first in on the story when it breaks, you give me what you've got.'

'All right. And thanks. About that fire, nobody's making any statements. But a tip from inside the fire service is that arson's been confirmed. No guns seem to be missing, but there's a gangland connection 'though nobody's letting out what it is. Does that help?'

'It might,' Keith said. 'But don't print that.' He hung up.

His other call was to the Strathclyde police. It took a few minutes of argument and of being switched from extension to extension before he found himself speaking to Superintendent Gilchrist. Keith had once done Gilchrist a favour and never allowed him to forget it.

'You're working late,' Keith said.

'When did I ever not?' said the superintendent's clipped voice. 'And what's this enquiry of yours about last night's fire?'

Keith was familiar with the need to give some information before collecting in return. The rule was to give as little and to get as much as possible. 'Have you seen the evening paper?' he asked.

'When do I get time to read evening papers?'

Keith sighed. It was time to stop conversing entirely in questions. 'I'm looking into the murder of Mary Spalding, near Aberdeen,' he said. 'The case against the accused was found not proven and his employers aren't too happy about it. It seems possible that there was a substitution of guns. A gunshop in Aberdeen burned shortly after the murder. Now another one in Glasgow goes up, just after I've pointed out to the High Court that, if the gun had ever belonged to the defendant, it had certainly been in use by somebody else between times. So I'm wondering whether somebody's trying to eradicate traces of his possession of that gun.'

There was a pause while Gilchrist thought it over. Keith looked again at the notes in front of him.

'Somebody will be up to see you within the next day or two,' Gilchrist said suddenly. 'Where are you staying?'

'Gregor's Hotel,' Keith said. 'Your friends in Aberdeen won't go much on the idea, you understand. It makes them wrong.'

'We'll make up our own minds,' Gilchrist said. 'All I'm prepared to tell you at the moment is that, if you're right, the man you're after has money and is using it to hire professional help. The arson was a skilled job, but the fire officer was experienced enough to be suspicious of a fragment of mechanism when he came across it. He brought it to us, and the m.o. was recognised. A professional arsonist, brought up from the Smoke. He was still in Glasgow and we found him lying low in a small hotel.

'He's saying nothing. And very wisely, because it seems likely that he was working for Harry Snide.'

Keith had heard the name. 'Ouch,' he said.

'You're right,' Gilchrist said. 'Probably more right than you realise. Snide has got bigger and cleverer during the last few years. Professional hard men, killers included. Some robbery, but mainly hiring out for intimidation or murder. We'd love to put him away, but all we ever get our hands on is his muscle. And even then a top-money brief turns up to give them the best possible chance of an acquittal. Some we win, of course. We sent down two of his men a couple of years ago. McHenge and Galway. When they came out, Snide sent them up to be based permanently in Aberdeen – partly, I suppose, to keep them out of our way, but mostly because Aberdeen's where most of the dirty money is these days. If you run into them, turn round and run the other way. They're not only rough, they're slick as well.'

Keith swallowed. Shennilco was not paying him enough. 'How will I know them?' he asked.

'Galway's a large, smiling, Irish type with a snub nose, bald as an egg. McHenge is smaller, dark and hatchet-faced. That,' Gilchrist said, 'is just off the top of the head. If you'd like to call me again tomorrow I'll have better descriptions.'

There was a silence on the line.

'Thanks,' Keith said. 'I don't like what you've told me, but thank you for telling it.'

'A pleasure. But if you learn anything which I ought to know, you pass it straight on. You hear me?'

'I do indeed,' Keith said. 'And the same to you.'

He hung up thoughtfully. He was making progress and yet the road was getting worse and its end more remote. If professional hit-men were involved, Hugh Donald's innocence was going to be very difficult to prove.

He dictated for half an hour, bringing his notes up to date. But silence and solitude were making him uneasy. He left the cassette on top of the typewriter where Sheila would find it first thing in the morning. Then he locked up the office and walked back to Gregor's Hotel, staying carefully among the bright lights and avoiding doorways.

At the reception desk a note was waiting for him. Radio Northsound hoped that he would agree to be interviewed. Keith dropped it into one of the bronze ash-trays. Two reporters, from rival papers, were also awaiting him and were less easily disposed of. He gave them his short list of names and referred them to Shennilco's PR department.

Too many ideas were buzzing in his head. They collided and confused each other. He put them firmly out of his mind while he ate a light dinner, only to have them flutter back when Jeremy Prather dropped into the other chair at his table and puffed smoke at him. The solicitor still looked sprucer than usual, but he had backslid in the matter of cigarette ash. There was also egg on his tie and a new burn on his lapel.

'I was just going to order coffee,' Keith said. 'Have you come to join me?'

'Have it in the lounge,' Jeremy said. 'There's somebody I want you to meet.'

Keith signalled for his bill. 'Who is it?' he asked.

'An accountant. I've spent most of the day finding the right person to talk to,' Jeremy said irritably. 'And asking the police stupid questions about a dead rabbit, for God's sake! They still have it, by the way, but they're not sure where exactly. I was supposed to be fixing up a divorce for a couple of my own clients. Well, they'll just have to learn to rub along together a little longer.'

Keith signed his bill and they walked downstairs together. A stout individual with a pale face and pig's eyes, and wearing a bold, pinstripe suit, was waiting for them. At that hour, custom had moved to the bars and dining room and the lounge was almost empty. Piped music secured the privacy of the corner table. They ordered coffee.

'Our friend would prefer to remain anonymous,' Jeremy said. 'You could probably identify him if you wanted to, but he'd just as soon stay nameless. He can tell you what you want to know, but after that, you've never seen him in the street.'

'Fair enough,' Keith said. He guessed that the stout man was, for a few minutes, on Shennilco's payroll.

'You want to know about Mary Spalding,' the stout man said. His accent, Keith thought, was Yorkshire, possibly Bradford. His voice whined.

'That's right,' Keith said. 'The Computer Queen.'

'That's what they called her, and she earned the name. She was a bloody well qualified accountant although she had an even better degree in computing. But she made fuller use of her expertise than most of us dare to do.'

The stout man glanced suspiciously at a pair of elderly ladies at the far end of the room and lowered his voice before going on. 'There's a hell of a lot of money circulating in the oil industry, Mr Calder,' he said. 'Firms working for firms who are working for other firms, all going after the big expenditure of the oil companies. Everything from a new platform to a year's supply of bread rolls. Contracts are being let by the hundred, and everybody wants the business. You know what that means?'

'Slush funds?' Keith said.

'To put it crudely, yes. Sweeteners. Happens all the time. A present to a buyer in exchange for a favour. That seems innocent enough. But then you get the bribes to other people's employees to buy commercial information. Not so much technical secrets, I don't mean that, though it happens. The big money goes for advance information on how much the rival firm is going to bid for the contract they both want.

'The oil companies are mostly above and beyond that sort of thing. Their slush funds are more likely to go to governments, to swing legislation their way. The other big operators, the rig constructors, shipping companies and so on, they do their accounting in-house and have their offices de-bugged once a month. But the smaller man uses an outside accountant. And he wants a bit more than the usual balance-sheets and tax-returns. He wants to be able to ask his accountant, "How much can I afford to bid for this contract?" and also, "How much can I afford to pay out in bribes, so's I can find out how much the others are going to bid? And how do I cover up the cost of the bribes?" So most firms of accountants, whether they know it or not, have a member who can answer that sort of question. You follow me?'

'I'm right with you,' Keith said. 'But surely his own estimator can tell him how much to bid?'

'His estimator can tell him the net cost. His accountant tells him what overheads he's got to allow for. Which makes the accountant the best person to buy the information off. You still with me?'

Keith nodded. 'Mary Spalding was selling her clients' secrets?'

'Such things happen all the time,' the stout man admitted. 'But she'd gone a whole lot further. If you

71

think of her as a broker, you'll get the picture. Clients were coming to her personally, because it was known that, whatever they wanted to know, she'd do the whole package for them – buy the information, figure out the bidding, cover up the bribes and present a nice series of accounts at the end of the day.'

'And could they trust her not to sell their information on again?' Keith asked.

'If they did,' the stout man said, 'they were out of their bloody minds.'

The stout man left after exchanging significant nods with Jeremy Prather. The solicitor suggested a drink. Keith felt that he owed him that much of the companionship which he seemed to crave. And it would save time in the morning if Keith reported the findings of the day. This he did over a pint for himself and a large whisky for Jeremy in the quietest bar, laying stress on the presence of two very hard men on the opposing team.

Jeremy was more interested in attack than in defence. 'We're beginning to see a very definite picture,' he said.

'True. But it's not a picture I like very much,' Keith said. 'One of the men – presumably McHenge, being the smaller man and so the easier to be mistaken for Hugh Donald at a distance – did the killing. But with a professional killer acting for the man with the motive, how do we prove a damn thing?'

'We'll figure out something when we know who his client is,' Jeremy said.

'Maybe. Until then, stay out of dark alleys.'

'I always do.'

'Don't look for me this time tomorrow,' Keith said. 'I think I'll have to go courting.'

'Miss Carlogie? Sooner you than me.'

'Who else? Mary Spalding kept records at home.

Somebody burgled the bungalow and took all her papers away. Then he, or somebody else, tried to repeat the visit, but by that time Miss Carlogie had installed the latest and best alarms. It's a reasonable inference that the real crunch document may still be there. Or, at least, our somebody thinks it is.'

'It's a wonder there hasn't been another fire,' Jeremy said.

'That's right,' Keith said, much struck. 'It is. If there's some nut around who thinks he can purge his past mistakes with fire, and if he or his goons have twice failed to find whatever-it-is, why didn't he try fire again?'

'Suggestions,' Jeremy said. 'Either he didn't want to destroy it, he wanted to have it. Or else he thought that it was so well tucked away that the risk of anyone finding it was less than the risk of drawing attention to the pattern of fires by starting another one.'

'Good points, both of them,' Keith said.

'I'm not just an ugly face. Are you ready for the other half?'

'In a minute. First I must go and wrestle with a python. That first one's pressing on my bladder.'

Rather than risk ambush in the hotel toilet Keith decided to go up to his room. The key was already in his pocket. He went up in an empty lift. No Glasgow tearaways were lurking in the corridor. He put his key in the door, hesitated, and then laughed at himself for jumping at shadows. Even so, after pushing the door open he stepped into the room quickly and sideways, flicking on the light as he went by.

The vicious slam as the door flung shut missed him by an inch. He found himself face to face, in the cramped area between the bedroom wall and the bathroom door, with Galway. The man was wearing a cloth cap, but if his snub nose had not identified him

Keith would have known by his size and by the merciless eyes.

'This here's a warning,' Galway said and jumped at him.

If Keith had not prepared himself mentally, he would have been caught and slammed against the bathroom partition, there to be held and pulped by the obviously stronger man. And if he had been more hasty, Galway would have died. Keith's counter-move was ready in his mind and he was stabbing with straight fingers before he could think.

In mid-blow, Keith changed his mind. It may have been that Galway's words sank in and he realised that the man had come with a warning rather than with murderous intent. At least in part it was an awareness that the death of Miss Spalding's killer would be the end of Hugh Donald's hopes. Whatever the reason, Keith turned his hand and delivered a paralysing chop to the point where the other's neck met his shoulder, stabbed the fingers of his other hand to the solar plexus and followed up, as Galway's head came forward, with a vicious hook to the side of the jaw.

The man's fall shook the room. Shaking with reaction and nursing his hand, Keith looked down. The cap had fallen off, exposing a hairless scalp. Keith nodded to himself.

Galway was still breathing, after a fashion. The man was probably not out for long. There was no time to waste.

That reminded him. His first need was becoming urgent. He relieved himself. Then he fetched from his suitcase the pair of white cotton gloves which always travelled with him. Their more usual function was to save the blueing of guns from his acid fingerprints. Gloved, he went through the man's pockets.

He found a driving licence in the name of Galway,

which was gratifying until he found three others in different names. Some cash. Several keys. A grubby handkerchief. A packet of cheap cigars. Matches.

Keith's pockets always held a supply of polythene bags which he used for occasional, unexpected gifts or acquisitions of game. Into one of the bags he dropped Galway's pocket diary and some scraps of paper. He returned everything else to the man's pockets. He almost missed one item, a brass knuckleduster on the man's right hand. If he had known that that was there, he might not have been so gentle. He decided to leave it in place. It would look well when the police arrived.

At his own request Keith was moved to another bedroom, comfortingly closer to the main comings and goings of the hotel, and in it he managed to sleep. But between the enquiries of the police into the night and those of more senior officers the following morning, he had little time to think about Hugh Donald's troubles.

Only one sequence stayed in his mind. At police headquarters between King and Queen Streets (and still referred to as Lodge Walk), a chief inspector, whose name Keith soon forgot, asked him whether he knew the man.

'I'd never seen him before,' Keith said.

'Do you know who he is?'

There was no avoiding the question. 'I can guess.'

'How?'

'I spoke to Superintendent Gilchrist at Strathclyde. He warned me about two hard cases who were in Aberdeen. This sounds like one of them.'

'And what else did this Superintendent Gilchrist tell you?'

'Phone him.'

'I'm asking you.'

'Are you going to take my word for it?'

'I'm not that daft.'

Keith's hesitation before he replied did nothing to improve the atmosphere. 'Then why should I waste my breath?'

He was put out of the office while a call was made to Superintendent Gilchrist. Afterwards, the chief inspector was even less friendly.

'So you think that there was a substitution of guns in the Spalding case?'

'You know I do,' Keith said patiently. 'I said so in the High Court, and got quoted in all the papers.'

'And you think two different gunshops have been fired, to cover it up?'

'I thought that the possibility was worth looking into.'

'Well, it isn't.'

Keith's temper was beginning to go. 'That's very useful and interesting,' he said. 'On what do you base that conclusion?'

The chief inspector refused to be drawn. 'You think that somebody sent this man to warn you off?'

'What the hell else? I'd be interested to hear any other explanation.'

'He says that you attacked him in the corridor and must have dragged him into your room while he was unconscious. He denies uttering any threat or warning.'

'And I suppose I put the knuckleduster on his fist?'

'That's what he suggests.'

'Gilchrist will have told you his record, if you didn't already know it,' Keith said. 'In the face of that, believe what you want to believe.'

He was free by lunch-time without having to invoke a solicitor or even refer to his legal rights. But he had an unpleasant suspicion that official help from the city police had become even less likely than before.

At two, he walked into Jeremy Prather's office. Sheila was typing a legal letter on the solicitor's notepaper.

'You don't have to do that,' Keith said.

'I don't mind, when there's nothing else happening. I hate sitting idle. There are spare keys to Mr Prather's flat here. Do you think he'd mind if I did some cleaning and tidying?'

'Probably.'

'Too bad! What's this we hear about a fight in your room at the hotel?'

'Just that. You'll read all about it when you come to type up my notes. I'll dictate them now. Is Jeremy's room empty?'

'He went out with his policeman contact. And a right pair of oddballs they make! He said he'd probably be the rest of the afternoon.'

'And Hugh Donald?'

'He turned up for your meeting this morning,' Sheila said. 'Mr Prather told him what had happened and warned him that another man might still be on the warpath. Mr Donald thinks that the other man may have been watching him last night, because he saw a small and hatchet-faced man talking to one of the guards on the Shennilco gate, and the same man or one just like him was outside his house when he got home. Mr Prather told him to be careful and to stay out of dark alleys.'

'That's what I told Mr Prather,' Keith said.

'And they've got the shotgun back from the police. It's on Mr Prather's desk.'

'I'll take a look at it. And give me an outside line to Jeremy's phone, please.'

Keith carried the tape-recorder through and took possession of Jeremy's desk and chair. Ignoring the temptation of the gun, because its time was not ripe, he telephoned to the hotel near Kemnay and invited Jenny Carlogie to dine with him. She sounded delighted and promised to book a table.

He brought his notes up to date, and only then allowed himself to pick up the Armas Alicante gun which he had last handled in the witness-box. He found a small magnifying glass in Jeremy's desk and studied the gun minutely, adding his findings to the tape as he went along.

A lot could be learned from a gun about its owner. There was, of course, the risk that the gun had not been in the hands of the man behind Miss Spalding's death but had been known to him and stolen or acquired at the last minute; but the contingency was remote. Keith wished that he could have seen the gun when it was found, before many small indications had been removed along with such fingerprints as the gun might have carried. Well, the fingerprints would be on record.

Traces of rust showed. Some of these might be due to neglect by the police after a sojourn in the damp grass. But not all. And a well lubricated and protected gun should have withstood such treatment.

Keith habitually carried a small leather case containing a handle and a variety of differently sized turnscrew blades. He detached and withdrew the locks. Inside, the gun was a mess of congealed oil blackened with gunsmoke and with rust well established.

There was confirmation of its owner's heedlessness in the numerous dents and scratches in the stock. These could easily have been lifted or filled. There were scratches in the finish of the barrels and the stock was in dire need of linseed oil or wax.

One particular set of scratches, in the front of the trigger-guard and adjacent on the bottom plate, interested him. The man had been in the habit of hanging

78

his gun on a fence before getting over.

The handle for his turnscrews was tapered and marked for gauging the muzzles of shotguns. He found that the chokes were as they had been when the gun left the makers. They would have thrown a very tight pattern. Keith knew that the makers had supplied them thus because it was easier and cheaper to remove choke than to add it. The man had not bothered. Yet the gun showed signs of much use. So either he had not cared whether he hit or missed, which would make him unusual to the point of being unique, or else he was an excellent shot whose aiming errors were less than the small spread of the patterns. That he had had the gun altered to fit him but had not had the chokes altered supported the assumption.

The interiors of the barrels were still perfect except for a haze of tiny pits extending for a few inches in front of the chambers. Keith had seen this disfigurement often on old guns but rarely in modern ones. Good modern cartridges have anti-corrosive primers, but cheaper, imported cartridges of dubious origin may still have corrosive, fulminate primers. So the man had been in the habit of buying 'bargain' cartridges, probably in bulk and by post.

Prolonged and frequent contact between fingers and the finish of gun-barrels will remove some of the delicate blueing and leave a slight, silvery sheen. Keith found such traces. He guessed that his man had not been in the habit of wearing gloves while shooting. Most men hold a gun with the aiming hand at the front of the fore-end; but on this gun the sheen was clear of the fore-end and on the barrels alone. Its user, then, had had very long arms or had used an old-fashioned, straight-armed posture reminiscent of King George V. The worn area seemed to be more extensive on the left side of the barrels than on the right, suggesting, again, the left-handed user. But of this he could not be quite sure.

He stood up and mounted the gun to his right shoulder and then to his left. There seemed to be little difference. In neither case could he quite align his eye with the rib without adopting attitudes which were almost inconceivable in the shooting field. The man must have a thin face with broad cheekbones and wide-set eyes. And young rather than old; during the ageing process, the point in the eye from which vision is centred moves fractionally inward towards the nose.

The gun felt wrong in another way. Because the cushioning of the rubber recoil-pad blurred his sensations it took him some seconds to recognise the discrepancy. The toe of the butt was catching him lower than he liked. The gun's owner must have a flatter chest than himself or he would have suffered bruised muscles.

He concentrated for another hour without finding any more clues to the user of the gun. But these were ample. Keith felt that he would almost know the man if he passed him in the street. He would know him at a glance if he saw him shooting. But where to go? Keith wondered whether he could enlist the aid of the local wildfowling and clay pigeon clubs. One of their members would surely recognise such a description.

When he gave up at last, Sheila had already left for the night. There was a note to say that Jeremy Prather would not be back. He had gone to Lodge Walk in pursuit of the missing rabbit and also in the faint hope of persuading the police to oppose an application for bail which had been made on behalf of Galway.

It was already dark when Keith walked, by the best-lit route, to fetch his car from the long-term car-park where it waited for him. He was earlier than he had intended and he paused along the way to do some impulse shopping. The car started reluctantly after its short hibernation. He gave it a few minutes to warm up before he set off.

There had been a slight thaw during the day, but the frost had returned with night and a fresh sprinkling of snow lay over the new ice. In places the roads were like skid-pans, but salt and sand helped the traffic to keep going with only an acceptable minimum of accidents.

Despite the conditions, Keith decided to heed Hugh Donald's words and to take the Skene road. Even there, the traffic was not light and he was clear of the city before he was sure that another car was following. This came as no surprise. With Galway removed, he had been expecting McHenge to take an interest. Walking the streets, he had stayed with the crowds and watched his back.

He slowed suddenly and the pursuing car came closer before its driver reacted and dropped back. The lights of an oncoming car showed Keith only a pale blob, but, as the lights went by, the blob was dramatically side-lit for one useful instant. Holding onto the memory, Keith was sure that he had detected a hatchet face over a pale scarf.

He watched and pondered. He was soon sure that the other driver was either unskilled or driving a car which was strange to him. Skene, and his turning for Kemnay, came up but Keith drove on towards Alford. His one advantage was that his car felt as familiar to him as his shoes. He turned on the speed, passing car after car whenever the oncoming traffic allowed. He came up behind a gritting lorry. Horns blared and lights blazed as he passed it in the gap between two buses and ran onto a surface which would not have shamed an ice-rink. He kept going, catching each slide with a flick of the wheel or kicking the tail out with a burst of power. It was delicate work in the dark and on a road only half-remembered, but he survived. Soon McHenge, if it were he, was half a mile behind and lost among other vehicles.

Keith turned right at Tillyfourie and came back towards Kemnay through Monymusk. For the last few miles he had the road to himself.

SEVEN

Jenny Carlogie had come off duty but, Keith noted with amusement, she was waiting in the manager's office so that she could make an entrance a minute or two after his arrival. She had abandoned her Angora and tweeds for a pretty frock and had made up for the loss of her jewels, 'such as they were', by the purchase of some costume jewellery discreet enough to pass for real at first glance. She came out smiling and her smile was bright with happiness.

She surprised him by being good company, ready with bright if shallow chatter, flatteringly willing to listen to his own opinions. Over drinks and an excellent dinner, they avoided the topics of the murder and of the missing inheritance. The bill made Keith's eyebrows go up. He filed the receipt away carefully in his wallet for the Shennilco accountant to worry over.

It was Keith who remembered to load her bicycle into the rear of his hatchback. It seemed that Miss Carlogie was already trusting him to chauffeur her to work in the morning.

The hotel staff had been curious about Miss Carlogie's gentleman friend. The moving car gave them their first chance to talk in privacy.

'I've been thinking some more about your burglar. If he tried to come back, he can't have got what he wants,' Keith said. 'You've had no more ideas about where your friend's money could have vanished to?'

'None at all.'

'Would you like me to try to help?'

'I wish you would,' she said.

'You realise that you'd have to trust me?'

'If you tricked me,' she said, 'I'd be no worse off than I am now. But I don't think you would.' She put a hand through his arm.

'There's another thing. If the money was dirty, if it had been obtained by embezzlement . . . had you thought of that?'

'Yes, of course.' She sounded surprised that he should doubt it.

'It might only be possible to give it back and claim a reward. Probably ten per cent. It could still be a lot of money, but not as much as she wanted you to have.'

'We'll share, half and half,' she said comfortably.

They were coming to the big sycamore tree. Keith slowed and parked where Hugh Donald had parked the day before. 'You remember seeing the man coming down the gulley here, the day Mary Spalding died?'

'It was only for a second,' she said.

'I know that. But even in a second, you must have got some impression. Was he a big man? Or small and hatchet-faced?'

She concentrated, perhaps searching her recollection, possibly absorbing his suggestions. 'He was thin,' she said. 'Hatchet-faced would just describe him.'

Keith sighed with relief. He would much prefer that McHenge, who was already established in his own mind as the killer, had also returned with the cheque book and been seen by Jenny Carlogie. One strong case would be better than two shaky ones.

His sigh pulled her towards him and they kissed. She seemed to expect it. Her lips were eager. Keith, who would rather have been kissing his wife, was only mildly stirred, but when it was over she could hardly draw breath. 'Let's go home,' she said.

Obligingly, Keith started the car. They drove in silence, but thoughts were flickering between them like an electric discharge.

He came to the side road which passed her bungalow. They left behind the tracks of many cars, with tarmac showing through the snow where the wear had been greatest. One set of tyre tracks still ran on ahead. 'You've had a visitor,' Keith said. But when he turned in through her gate, the tracks went on.

'Where does your side road lead to?' he asked as he pulled up at her front door.

'Nowhere. Just an old sand–pit.'

'Somebody went up there and he didn't come down again. I was followed this evening but I shook him off. He must have guessed where I was coming.'

'Leave him be,' she said. 'He can't get in to us if I set the alarms.'

'I'd rather know where he is,' Keith said. 'I don't want a bomb under my car or a bullet when I come out. You go in and make us a drink. If anyone but me comes to the door, set the alarms off and I'll come running. He'll have seen our lights, but he'll probably wait for us to settle. If he's watching from up near the sand-pit, how can I get near without being seen?'

'Go round the other side of the bungalow,' she said, 'and round the first field. The field's higher in the middle. You can't see across it. Be careful,' she added.

'You sound like a wife,' he said. Immediately, he would have recalled the remark if he could. Mention of a wife could spoil the mood of a romantic tryst.

The night was clear but dark. The snow reflected and magnified what little light the stars let fall. He wished that he could have borrowed white clothing, a painter's overalls. He was wearing good, leather boots, but the snow was deep enough in places to reach his calves and soon his feet were damp. He found a gate in the garden wall and set off round the field.

The tracks could have been made by the return of a car which had been in the sand-pit during the last snowfall. He hoped very much that he was wasting his time.

It was twenty minutes' walk in the heavy going and all the way the middle of the field hogged the skyline. Once a pair of partridges, unusually early in establishing squatter's rights to their chosen nesting territory, burst out of the hedge-bottom and made him jump.

As he covered the third side of the field, he seemed to be climbing and there was a low, broad hump on the skyline ahead. Keith stepped gently over a fence and climbed the slope. He would have given a lot to have had nails in his boots. He finished the climb on all fours and looked over the crest. Below him was the hollow of the sand-pit and to his left the roof and back of an estate car, facing towards the cottage. As far as he could see the car had no outside mirror on the left. Keith backed away and set off leftwards around the hump. He stumbled once over a hummock hidden in the snow and nearly fell.

Another short stalk brought him towards what he hoped was the blind side rear of the car. The ground was uneven under the snow, but Keith had the knack of going silently over difficult ground. He stole towards the back of the car. It was in darkness except for the glow of the radio although the headrests prevented him from seeing the driver's head.

He was almost up to the car and already planning how to give the driver the fright of his life when his eyes, now fully adjusted to the darkness, saw footprints leaving the car. As far as he could make out, they did not return. Heart in mouth, he span round.

He had been outmanoeuvred. A thin, hatchet-faced man – McHenge for a certainty – was coming up behind him, a self-loading pistol in his hand and pointing at Keith's chest.

McHenge was still ten yards off. At that range, only an expert would have half a chance of hitting a moving target in such bad light, and the Glasgow tough rarely troubles to practise marksmanship. Keith decided to stake all on a dive over the car.

The snow beat him. He decided afterwards that, where he was standing, it overlaid a frozen puddle. Whatever the reason, his frantic leap only shot his feet from under him and he fell heavily, winded. When he managed to raise his head, McHenge was standing over him. The pistol was steady on his guts.

'Too bad about you, Jimmy,' McHenge said. The Glasgow accent was very strong. He shone a light on Keith's face and then dropped the torch into his pocket. 'I got my orders today. You're next for the chop.'

'Orders from Harry Snide?' Keith asked. His voice tried to play tricks on him.

'Direct from the client. But don't fash me by asking who he is because I don't know. You can have it hard if you want it that way, but I'll give it you easy if you're good. What'd you do to Bob Galway?'

'I hardly touched him,' Keith said. The less McHenge feared him, the better his chances would be. 'He was waiting in my room. He swung at me and I pushed him in the chest and he went down. It must have been a heart attack.'

'Pull the other one. There was nothing wrong with Bob's heart. The quack in Barlinnie checked him over not six months back. On your feet, Jimmy, and face the car. I can connach you where you are,' he added, 'but I'd as soon you walked, and I've no doubt you'd want to live a little longer.'

Keith dragged himself to his feet and turned towards the car. Hope, which should have died at that moment, came alive. McHenge was making two mistakes. He let Keith stand upright when he should have made him lean against the car. And he pressed the pistol into the small of Keith's back while he patted his clothing for a weapon. Keith had seen the pistol. He knew the general type and had seen the protruding barrel; and Keith also knew that self-loading pistols will nearly always refuse to fire if backward pressure on the barrel locks the trigger. Nearly always. . . . But it was as good a chance as he was going to get. His fears were overwhelmed by a determination to survive.

Pushing off from the car, Keith span and chopped sideways. The gun fired as it flew out of the man's hand and again when it landed in the snow, but no damage was done. The two men grappled, chest to chest, slipped and went down together. McHenge probed for Keith's eyes. Keith rolled his head, tried vainly to use his knee and struck out blindly.

A lucky blow landed, not hard but squarely. McHenge rolled away and got to his knees. Keith started to scramble up, found that he had a good purchase with one foot and threw himself onto McHenge's back, locking one elbow round the man's neck and compressing the carotid arteries under the ears. McHenge kicked, groaned, weakened and suddenly went limp. Keith held on while he counted another five seconds and then let the other man fall back into the snow. He got shakily to his feet. In his memory he could still hear the whisper of death.

There was no time to waste; McHenge's sleep would only last a few minutes at the most. Keith took the torch from the unconscious man's pocket and went to look for the pistol. He shuddered when he found it, a Japanese Shiki Kenju Type 94 left over from World War II and quite the most dangerous service pistol ever made. If Keith had recognised it, he might not have dared take the risk. But ignorance had been more than bliss, it had been salvation.

The torch showed him no convenient length of rope in the back of the car. He was sure that there was none in his own. Not even a piece of string. He thought of bootlaces, but McHenge's boots were zipped up the side and he was damned if he was going to sacrifice his own. He patted his pockets and found that he was still carrying one of the purchases which he had made earlier in the day. A slow grin spread over his face.

He loaded the smaller man without difficulty into the passenger seat of the estate car and pulled off his boots and socks. Then he squeezed Superglue onto the palm of McHenge's left hand and pressed the palm against the sole of the right foot. The glue took hold almost instantly. He repeated the process, right hand to left foot.

The keys were in the dash. Keith brushed the snow off his clothes, settled into the driver's seat and set off towards the bungalow. By his side, McHenge snored contentedly.

McHenge was already beginning to yawn and blink when Keith parked the estate car between his own car and the living room window. He left the engine running. The lights were on in the bungalow, spilling a swathe of light which made his tasks easier. He tossed McHenge's boots and socks onto the back seat and made sure that the tube of solvent was safe in his pocket.

'What—?' said McHenge. He tugged at his hands. '—the hell?' he finished. He twisted his head and transfixed Keith with a sizzling glare.

89

'Not much fun being on the losing side, is it?' Keith said. 'Now, listen to me you lethal turd. You killed Mary Spalding and you were going to kill me.'

McHenge began to protest his innocence and good intentions, but Keith broke in and McHenge stopped to listen.

'You,' Keith said, 'are going to commit suicide in a fit of remorse. A piece of garden hose from the exhaust into the car is all it'll take. After I chauffeur you out into the wilds, use the solvent and put your boots and socks back on you, who's going to question it? Your only hope of living is to tell me who your client is.'

McHenge struggled again. His face darkened with effort and range, but he remained fast. 'You'd not,' he said.

'I bloody would,' Keith said. 'Why wouldn't I?'

'I don't know the bloody client! I tell you.'

'You'll have to do better than that,' Keith said. He put his hand on the door handle. 'You said you got your orders direct from the client. Last chance. Once I've fetched a piece of hose, I shan't feel like changing my mind. I'd hate the effort to go to waste.'

The argument may have rung a bell with McHenge who was already demoralised by his position. 'I tell you I don't,' he said shrilly. 'Listen. He kens my hotel. He'd send me notes. Once he wrote me to meet him, but outdoors and in the dark. And . . .'

'That's when he gave you the shotgun?'

McHenge hesitated, rolling his eyes around. But he was in his own car and there was no sign of a recording device. 'That's right,' he said.

'And the rabbit?'

'Aye, it was. But I didn't see him, just the shape of a tall claes–pole and the sound of his voice.'

'What sort of a voice?'

'Nothing special. Much like you'd hear on the

wireless. Maybe deeper than some. The rest of my orders came through Harry Snide. That's all I know, so help me!'

'You can do better, to save your foul neck. Last chance.'

'If I knew more, I'd tell you.' McHenge groaned. 'I'd not be put down for the like of him. But I never got sight of him. I wanted to see him, just for future reference. It could've been useful, later.'

'Blackmail,' Keith said.

'I wouldn't do that,' McHenge said. 'Self-protection, that's the term. I took out a fag an' asked had he got a light. But he wasn't that daft. Handed me a box of matches and told me no' to strike one until he was away.'

'If that's the best you can do . . .' Keith said. He tried to invest the words with special menace. He twisted the door handle.

'It's all there is,' McHenge said desperately. 'Except . . . I could smell something on him.'

'Like what?'

'Not much, me being a smoker myself. But I thought I smelled cigar smoke.'

Keith pursued his questions for a few more minutes, but he was satisfied that he had all that the man could tell him. He gave up.

Very carefully, so as not to be joined to McHenge in unholy deadlock, Keith squeezed Superglue onto the man's lower lip. 'You can close your mouth now,' he said.

'You can't do this to ne,' McHenge protested, keeping his mouth as far open as he could.

'Believe me, I'm doing it,' Keith said. He put a hand to McHenge's ear and twisted it.

'You b—' McHenge began and stopped dead. His eyes bulged.

91

'That's better,' Keith said. He skimmed through McHenge's pockets and stowed away his findings for later study. 'I don't owe you a damn bit of goodwill. Annoy me once and I'll glue one of your nostrils shut. Annoy me again and I'll glue up the other one, and you can learn to breathe through your ears or snuff it, the choice'll be yours.

'I'm going to leave you here while I go inside. I'm leaving the engine ticking over so that you'll not freeze, but I'm damn sure you won't be able to drive. If you're very clever, you might manage to get out of the car. But not without making a noise. And I'll be looking out from time to time. Try anything like that and I'll take your breeks down and glue your bum to the bonnet of the car, and you can ride in to Aberdeen that way. Got the idea?'

Without waiting for an answer, he got out, slammed the car's door and went into the bungalow.

Jenny Carlogie was waiting in the hall, wringing her hands in apprehension. When she saw Keith she seemed to resume breathing.

'I caught him,' Keith said. 'He's sitting in his car outside. And he'll stay there.'

'You're sure?'

'I'm in no doubt of it.'

'Is he tied up?'

'Something like it. Forget him.'

She turned her attention to Keith. 'You're soaking wet,' she said. 'You'd better take those things off. Only I've nothing to lend you while they dry.'

'It's warm in here,' Keith said. 'I don't mind if you don't.'

She nodded. He could almost see her thoughts in a little balloon above her head as she wondered whether she should pretend to be scandalised and decided not to

92

risk spoiling the intimacy of the moment. He stripped to his underpants. She hung his clothes in an airing cupboard and then came and and stood close to him.

'Before we let anything distract us,' Keith said, 'let's look for the answer to your problem.'

'All right,' she said.

'Show me her part of the house.'

She led him through into a large room, evidently made by throwing two rooms together, and closed the curtains. It had been furnished as a combined bedroom, sitting room and office, all in a severely masculine style. At the far end from the bed, a whole wall had been given over to a large desk and fitted cupboards. On the desk sat a small computer flanked by a disc drive, printer and video screen all linked by flat multiple cables.

'Knowing her as you did,' Keith said, 'would she be more likely to keep her confidential records on paper or on the computer?'

'She never trusted anything to paper,' Jenny said. 'She always destroyed any notes as she went along.'

'That's what I thought. I'd guess on disc. Your visitors thought so too if they took her gramophone records. Did she have any cassettes of music?'

'They took those too.'

'And still they came back. They must have listened to a hell of a lot of music before they found that there wasn't any electronic blippery there.' Keith thought for a moment. Jenny was darting little glances at him. It distracted him. He sucked in his stomach. A large bookcase held a mixture of novels and textbooks. They looked too neat. 'Did they go through her books?' he asked.

'They were all tumbled on the floor. I put them back.'

'If she was going to hide away her records,' Keith said, 'she'd surely have left you some clue. Did she ever

93

say anything about it which sounded in the least bit off-beat?'

'Not that I remember.'

She was giving her attention to him but not to the problem.

Keith, while admitting to a wild and rakish past, considered himself now to be a reformed character. Indeed, ever since the birth of his daughter had forced him to review his moral values, he felt that he had been a model of marital fidelity. But it would have been against his nature and his inclination to allow new-found scruples to interfere with his much older enthusiasm for the pursuit of truth. He wondered whether he could coax Jenny Carlogie a little further without quite surrendering his precarious virtue.

He assessed her out of the corner of his eye. Had he misread her? Perhaps a little flirtatious and suggestive badinage would satisfy her for the moment. 'Fully dressed like that,' he said, 'you make me feel naked.'

He expected her to bridle, but she leaped at the suggestion. 'I wouldn't want that,' she said. With the faintest pretence of modesty she slipped out of her dress and dropped it over a chair. In seconds, her state of undress matched his own. Her figure was good but not, he thought, a patch on Molly's. She came and leaned against him. He was left in no doubt that she expected him to take her then and there, but he guessed that once love-making began her attention would be bespoken indefinitely.

He patted her haunch in what he hoped was a brotherly way. 'Think hard,' he said. 'What did she say?'

She rubbed herself against him in silence for a few distracting seconds. Just when he thought that her mind was away, she proved him wrong. Evidently the pull of money was as strong as the pull of sex. 'There was only one thing she ever said and I don't think it'll be much help. Just after she told me that she'd made a will in my favour, she said that the money had my name on it. She seemed to want to laugh about it. I thought that she was just saying the same thing again in a different way, but now I'm not so sure.'

'You're probably right,' Keith said. 'That may not be much help until after we've found it.' During his preoccupation, his hand had become more affectionate. He pulled it up to the small of her back and then pushed her gently away. 'We'd better take a look around,' he said.

'If we must,' she said. 'Let's get it over and done with. What are we looking for? One of her floppy discs?'

'That's my guess, if it's not on a cassette. Probably in a thin envelope about four inches square. It'll be carefully hidden, but not anywhere it could get damaged. It could be taped to the underside of a drawer or shelf, or under the lining paper or the clothes in a drawer. Would it be in this room?'

'I'm sure it would,' she said. 'I did all the house-keeping, but this was her own place.'

'Let's make a start, then.'

They searched. Once or twice Keith went through to the living room to look out at McHenge, but the man was only sitting and glowering out, just able to see over the dashboard.

Concentration was difficult. Wherever he turned Keith found that he was aware, through the corner of his eye, of a well-rounded and silk-girt buttock or a bobbing breast and he knew that she was equally aware of him. She seemed content for the moment, and he thought that she was finding her own erotic stimulus in moving around, provocatively short of naked, in the presence of a man whose arousal must be almost painfully obvious.

After half an hour, much discouraged, Keith stood

95

looking at the bookcase. 'Did it seem that they'd given all the books a shake?' he asked.

She looked round from examining the backs of pictures. 'That's just how it seemed.'

'Then they wouldn't have missed—' Keith stopped dead.

'What is it?'

'Don't hold your breath, but I think I'm looking at it.' He reached up and took down a novel. *Poor Jenny* said the title. At each end, the bright dust jacket had been taped. He ripped the tape off one end. A recess had been cut into the outside of the back cover. It held a black envelope about four inches square.

She looked at it in excitement. 'Can we try it in the computer?' she asked.

'Better not. I don't know much about these things, but I do know that confidential material can be protected. We might wipe off exactly what we want to know. I'll get an expert onto it tomorrow.'

'Whatever you say.' She was laying conscious emphasis on her own meekness.

Keith went once more to look out at McHenge. She followed him.

'He'll see you,' Keith warned.

'Let him,' she said. 'He can't be getting much other fun. Who is he? Do you think he killed Mary?' She sounded no more than mildly interested.

'It seems possible.' Keith pulled her away from the window before McHenge's furious eyes could pop right out of his head. 'He was certainly ready to kill me. I'll take him into Aberdeen and see how much of it we can prove.'

It had been Keith's intention, in keeping with the virtue which nowadays clung about him, to make his escape as soon as he had Mary Spalding's secrets in his hands. But just as his mind decided that the time had come for his departure he found that his body had reached quite a different decision. They had come too far to turn back. Besides, he felt that he owed it to her. Putting aside all thought of McHenge's uncomfortable vigil, he pulled Miss Carlogie to her late friend's bed.

He told himself that Molly would understand. The thought was less than comforting.

EIGHT

She managed to be voracious and demanding without
forsaking her subservient role, but they went well
together. Jenny made breakfast for him in the morning.
His clothes had dried, so he dressed before sitting down
to her eggs in a blue and white kitchen.

'One thing,' he said. 'If anyone ever asks, I caught
that man this morning, not last night. I wouldn't want it
known that I kept him prisoner in the car while you and
I . . .'

She looked up from her cornflakes and blushed, but
there was the shadow of a complacent smile. 'I
understand,' she said.

'And you'll remember?'

She nodded and turned her eyes away to the
snowbound scenery beyond the window. 'If we can find
the money,' she said dreamily, 'I'd still like to get away.
Somewhere warm, with somebody loving.'

Keith jumped. 'Not me,' he said. 'I'm a happily
married man.'

'Bless us, I wasn't meaning you,' she said, laughing.
'I don't think I'd like a man around all the time. Ladies
are gentler. Should I take that man out a cup of tea?'

'I don't think he could face it,' Keith said. He was
nettled. He thought that he had been wonderfully
gentle. 'Use my car to get to your work, if you can
drive. And may I use your phone before I go? It's a local
call.'

He made his phone call and then came back to her. 'Will you be coming back for your car?' she asked.

'Assume not. But I'll be in touch when I've done what I can about the information on the disc.'

'Yes, of course.'

She was not his sort of woman but it was impossible not to feel some tenderness. 'Goodbye, little female person,' he said.

'Perhaps it would be better if you didn't come back yourself,' she said in a very small voice. 'I don't want to be the sort of person who does that sort of thing. You understand?'

'I understand,' Keith said, knowing that it was only too true.

'Then goodbye, large male person.' She turned away.

McHenge was still squatting, helpless and sullen, glowering out with difficulty at an equally sullen morning. He made noises through his nose which Keith did not bother to try to interpret. The car's engine was still running but there was enough fuel left to take them where they were going.

At first, Keith drove in silence, depressed by his own frailty. He could forgive himself for his infidelity which had, after all, been in the line of duty. But he should not have enjoyed it. The change had been refreshing. This had not been his first infidelity to Molly, but the others had been with ladies whose favours he had known before his marriage so that no new precedent had been established. This time, he felt almost criminal.

But even a criminal gets time off for good behaviour. That was a cheering thought. Regarded in that light, his little lapse was no more than his just reward, a parole after years of faithful service. He brightened up and even told McHenge one or two mildly blue stories as they went along.

They headed towards Aberdeen over the Tyrebagger.

As Hugh Donald had warned, the traffic was heavy around Bucksburn and, when he turned off to the left, Keith found himself following a column to Dyce.

Hugh was waiting near the main gate of the airport. He slipped out of his coat and dropped it over the hunched figure of McHenge as he squeezed himself into the back seat.

'Drive on,' he said. He directed Keith through a secondary gate and onto a perimeter road. Muffled noises came from under the tweed coat.

A small helicopter was tucked away behind a hangar and here Keith halted the car. The pilot remained in his seat and stared blandly at the hangar wall.

'Too luxurious for this lout,' Keith said.

'We only keep a couple of executive choppers,' Hugh said. 'Our commercial flying's done by one of the big charter outfits.' He pulled the coat off McHenge. 'You think this is the hired killer?'

'I'm sure of it, but we can't prove it yet. What's the plan?'

'You said you wanted him salted away for a while. So we'll send him out to one of our rigs. The Operations Manager on Marina Beta is an Australian. His top crew have been with him for years and they're all intensely loyal. They'll keep him under wraps until we say otherwise. If we wanted, they'd lose him permanently.'

McHenge made honking sounds.

'He'll have to go on trial,' Keith said. 'We may not get as far as his client, but a prosecution of this animal for Mary Spalding's murder might get you off the hook.'

A rusty and battered Cortina pulled up behind them. Jeremy Prather got out and came to their nearside. 'So this is our killer,' he said. 'What's wrong with him?'

Keith would have liked to say that McHenge was a little stuck up, but he decided that the solicitor was in no

mood for feeble puns. 'Superglue,' he said. 'Don't
worry about him. He's immobilised until I use the
solvent on him.'

Jeremy looked closely at McHenge. 'I go along –
reluctantly – with your idea of stowing him away on a
rig,' he said. 'But you can't keep him like this. It isn't
human.'

'Nor is he,' Keith said.

'At least unglue his mouth.'

'You may regret it, but all right. Although what I
think he wants most is a pee. If we lift him into the
bushes, you can give him a little help.'

Jeremy looked at McHenge's useless hands. 'Let him
burst,' he said. 'But open his mouth.'

'OK. But I think it's a waste of our time and his
breath.'

Keith applied the solvent, using a rag from the car's
glove compartment. As McHenge's lips came free, he
was already speaking to Jeremy Prather. 'Hey, is it right
you're the lawyer? Tak' me on. I'm suing this bogger.
Kept me like this, shut in a car all night while he had it
awa' wi' the Carlogie wumman.'

'He's a liar,' Keith said. 'I only caught him an hour
ago.'

'He's the yin's the leear,' McHenge squawked. 'An'
Harry Snide'll gie youse a thousand quid if you'll phone
him an' say where they're sending me.'

'Tell me who your client is and I may be able to help
you.'

McHenge shook his head violently. 'My orders came
from Harry,' he said. 'D'you want my case, or will you
get me someone else?'

'You're right, it's a waste of time,' Jeremy said. 'If he
knows he won't tell us. Glue him up again.'

'I've used all the glue,' Keith said. 'And most of the
solvent.'

'There's a dozen chemists on the rig,' Hugh said. 'They can figure out how to unglue him. Let's load him up.'

'Right,' said Keith. 'You two take an ear each and I'll grab his balls.'

With a car apiece to be taken back to Aberdeen, there was no opportunity for discussion during the journey. Keith, less familiar with routes and lanes, lost time on the trip but managed to park the car near Jeremy's office. The other two, walking up from some remoter car-park, met him as he was locking up the car.

'You're on a yellow line,' Jeremy said. 'They'll tow it away.'

'Who cares?' Keith said. 'It's not my car and I've cleaned out any debris belonging to McHenge.' He was holding another of his polythene bags in one hand. From the other dangled McHenge's boots and socks. 'I forgot about these.'

Jeremy sighed. 'I'll see that they get out to him,' he said. 'You can give them to me . . . after we get back to my office.'

They fell into step.

'Did you manage what I wanted?' Keith asked.

'Sergeant Tooker should be here in a few minutes,' Jeremy said. 'You can say what you like to him. He won't report back until we tell him to. They're still searching for your rabbit.'

'If they decide to find it,' Keith said, 'get a tame pathologist to collect it from them.'

'I phoned your wife's cousin before I left for Dyce,' said Hugh. 'She's going to buy the computer you wanted.'

'With a bit of luck, I'll get to keep it,' the solicitor said.

'With a bit of money, you can buy it,' Hugh said.

'Bloody scrounger! And an expert from Shennilco will be on his way soon. Why did you want him? What other little treasures have you brought us?'

Keith glanced around. An old lady with a shopping bag might have been within earshot. 'You'll be amazed,' he said.

'Miss Carlogie co-operated? As if McHenge hadn't told us,' Hugh added. 'Greater love hath no man.'

'You don't want to believe all that bastard says, except when he thinks you'll kill him if he doesn't tell the truth. We know everything he knows, for what little it's worth. And we know what Miss Carlogie knows.'

'The bitch!' Jeremy said. 'She won't tell the defence solicitor a damn thing, and then she spills it all to the next man to come along.'

'If you've got it, you may as well use it,' Keith said. 'You should have changed your shirt and smiled.'

'I know what it was,' the solicitor said. 'She was hostile to me because I was defending the man she thought killed her friend.'

'She was very nice to me the other day,' Hugh said, grinning.

Jeremy sulked all the way up the stairs to his office.

They had hardly settled in Jeremy's outer office when there came a knock at the door, so casual that it might have been accidental, and Sergeant Tooker floundered into the room. He was, as Sheila had suggested, an unusual policeman and a good match for Jeremy Prather.

Tooker was tall, thin but pot-bellied, in a shabby and ill-fitting uniform. His hair was grey and the creases in his worn face were lined with silver stubble. He was not wearing socks. Keith learned later that, although the sergeant's lack of polish was a thorn in the flesh of his superiors, he was a valued member of the city police and

103

was frequently drafted onto CID work because of his inquisitive nose and an extraordinary affinity for gossip. Tooker could turn an interrogation into a cosy chat during which his victim would find himself divulging fragments of information which he had not even known that he knew.

Jeremy performed introductions and the sergeant shook Keith's hand firmly. 'Aye, man,' he said. 'I've been hearing a lot about you lately and no doubt I'll hear more. But, for the now, you'd best gie's your crack.' The three chairs being bespoken, he settled himself on the window sill and assumed that air of admiring attention with which he so often lulled the unwary into saying too much.

To an audience of three – four if the tape-recorder were included – Keith gave a neatly tabulated summary of his theory of Mary Spalding's murder and an expurgated account of recent events, truthful except that he allowed the search for the missing disc to occupy the whole night and transferred the attempt on his life and the capture of McHenge to the morning.

He finished, turned off the tape-recorder and switched to a less formal manner. 'This is the pistol,' he said, laying the weapon on the desk. 'I've unloaded it. There may still be some of his prints to be found. And here,' he produced three of his polythene bags, 'I have the odds and ends from Galway's pockets, the same from McHenge's, and what I could find in McHenge's car.'

'You realise,' Tooker said severely, 'that by sending yon lad out to the rig you've kept yourself from prosecuting him for the attack on yourself, or even using it in evidence in the other matter.'

'We knew that,' Jeremy said. 'But there was only Keith's word for it. And at least we've prevented him from walking out on bail like his friend and lousing up our attempts to find the man behind him.'

'There is that,' Tooker admitted. 'But these bits and pieces have lost value as evidence, being gathered up in this way. For a' that, we'll just get a wee bit of expert help. Most of our forensic work's done from Glasgow, but there's a lad I ken fine in the university, lectures in forensic science. We can see what he makes o' it a'. First, though, we'll just take a wee keek ourselves.'

He came and stooped over the desk. His fingers were surprisingly deft in manipulating the two ballpoint pens with which he sorted through the miscellaneous junk. The cigarettes and matches from McHenge's pockets seemed to interest him. He poked out the tray of matches, tilted the outer box to look inside and grunted sadly.

'To go by the notebooks of the officers who searched the place,' he said, 'there was an empty box of Bluebell matches found near the bottom of yon gulley. The inside was scorched, as if the mannie had the habit of sheltering his match from the wind by striking it and then holding it in the hollow end of the box. But no such luck!'

They were interrupted by the arrival of Sheila, accompanied by a youth to carry the boxes of computer hardware and followed by the boffin from Shennilco. The last arrival delighted Keith by being exactly what a boffin should be – bald and serious with thick spectacles. He answered to the name of Grenville. Hugh said later that not even the Shennilco Personnel Department had ever learned his first name if, indeed, he had one.

The others retired into the inner room while Mr Grenville set up the computer. Sergeant Tooker sat at the desk and resumed his search. Sheila produced a pair of tweezers which helped him greatly, but for the most part the search only revealed the sort of trivia which any man might collect. Galway's pocket diary contained a

105

list of expenditures which were presumably listed for reimbursement, but there was no significance to be found in them.

McHenge's wallet, however, made the sergeant's eyebrows climb slowly up his forehead. It held rather more cash than an honest man needs to carry, together with credit cards and driving licences in several different names.

'Galway's was the same,' Keith said. 'But I had to hand it over with him.'

'They could have held him on that alone if they'd wanted,' Tooker said. 'But your name's a dirty word just now – nae bogger likes being wrong – so they didn't oppose bail.' He used the tweezers to extract a folded slip of paper from the wallet and opened it with one of the pens. His eyebrows rose even higher and he whistled. 'Dinna' touch,' he said, 'but take a wee look at this.'

The commonplace, unlined paper carried a message printed neatly in block capitals with a black ballpoint pen: WATCH K.C. IF HE GETS WARM, COOL HIM. BURN THIS.

'He's a daft gyte to have kept it,' Tooker said. 'But if they was a' wise, we'd not catch any of them.' He looked at Keith. 'K.C. would be yourself?'

'Who else?' Keith said.

'Fairly that. M'hm. There's a faint imprint from the page above,' Tooker said, 'but damned if I can make anything o't. I'll get this to the forensic lad right away.' He got to his feet and stood silent for a moment, swaying from foot to foot. 'I'll awa' then.' But his eyes were on the boots behind the door. 'Damn it, that reminds me. Did those belong to McHenge? There was something about boots . . .'

'If there was,' Keith said, 'it didn't come out at the trial.'

106

'It'd not have seemed revelant. In a murder inquiry, ilka wee bit paper gets lifted, and there's aye plenty o't, folk being the heedless buggers that they are. And there's that much paper these days a man only has to pull out his snotterclout and he drops a piece. Well now, among all the scraps lifted from the farm where they found the body, there was a receipt from yin o' they grand stores around George Street. It was for a pair of black calfskin boots like these, and dated just twa days afore the murder. The lassie in the shop minded the sale fine and said she'd know the mannie again. A wee man, she said, wi' a thin face and a head so narrow you could slip it under a door.'

NINE

Mr Grenville, crossing with Sergeant Tooker in the inner doorway, announced that the computer was now in commission. But Keith paused before moving. 'We have a chance of proving that McHenge did the murder,' he said.

'Not good enough,' said Jeremy Prather. 'Convict a hired gun of the killing without implicating his employer and it may still be generally believed that he was hired by Hugh. And if we send him up the river alone, you can bet McHenge will implicate Hugh out of spite. We need the client.'

Keith shrugged. 'We still need luck,' he said. 'He's covered his tracks almost all the way, using a close-mouthed, hired killer who's never even seen his face. And we can't even make the most of what evidence we find. The police would have a team in sterile clothing picking it up into sealed bags and registering them from hand to hand into the laboratory and back. The way we're working, half our evidence may be inadmissable.'

'It's not forensic evidence that'll sink the client,' Jeremy said. 'What's more, Sergeant Tooker said something to the point. "Dod McHenge is a pro", he said. "He'll gie little away. Find me the client and a wee bittie of evidence, and in time he'll shop the both of them."'

'He could be right,' Keith said doubtfully. 'Let's see what else we can get.'

They gathered around the computer. Keith had brought the disc, still embedded in the novel for safety. He slipped it out and handed it to Mr Grenville.

'As I understand it,' Grenville said, 'you want me to get some highly confidential and possibly protected information off this disc. You're sure that this is the same hardware throughout?'

'As sure as I can be,' Keith said. Grenville's voice was pedantic and southern English, but Keith did not hold that against him. Some of his best friends were Englishmen.

'And I gather that the lady was a skilled programmer,' Grenville said thoughtfully. 'With this system it would be almost impossible to inbuild a protection against printing out but rather easier to embed a secret command to erase if given the wrong instruction. So first of all we'll use the printer to print out everything on the disc in its fundamental hexadecimal notation. What we call a hex dump. You follow me?'

Without waiting for the affirmative reply which he would not have received, he put the disc into the disc-drive, threaded the end of the computer paper into the printer and began keying in. The printer made zipping noises and the computer paper unfolded itself in a long chain which Sheila refolded neatly onto the wire rack. The video screen registered an incomprehensible jumble of letters and numerals.

After some minutes, when there was a stack of closely printed paper an inch thick on the rack, the printer stopped suddenly.

'Now,' Grenville said. 'At least if we lose it we have a hard copy and we can put it all back – at the expense of many hours of the most tedious work imaginable. Let's see what we've got.'

He keyed again. The video screen showed a menu and

then a short index of six file references. More keying and a summary of the accounts of one of Miss Spalding's clients appeared on the screen. 'I take it that this isn't what you're looking for?'

Jeremy Prather studied the figures, leaning forward and breathing heavily. 'The tax inspector might be more than just interested,' he said, 'but I don't think that we are.'

'Probably just a bland front,' said Hugh, 'to make Nosey Parkers like us think we've seen it all. Print it out anyway.'

In a few more minutes they had a print-out of the six sets of accounts. 'If there's anything for us here,' Jeremy said, 'I can't see it.'

'Those are the unprotected files,' said Grenville. 'From here on, it gets more difficult. The file names aren't on the catalog and she may have used an embedded command to erase if the wrong code is used. I suppose you've no clues as to what names she might have carried in her head?'

'Not the least idea,' Keith said. 'Presumably there's more to come. She wouldn't have hidden the disc so carefully just for a few mildly questionable accounts.'

'Of course there's more to come,' Grenville said impatiently.

'How could you possibly tell?'

'Because the hex dump was much too long for the little we've got out so far.' Grenville's voice held all the contempt of the expert for the tyro. 'Now, do we start trying the lady's initials or her birthday or what? Forwards or backwards? It's up to you.'

'Go back to the catalog,' Keith said.

Grenville touched the keys. The video screen flicked. It showed the bottom of the menu followed by a small panel of disc information, all negative. Below were the reference letters of the six files which they had already seen, arranged in two short columns of three.

'Let me try to understand,' Keith said. 'It's possible to file information without the file names appearing here?'

'Perfectly possible,' said Grenville. 'In fact, you can see that it's been done. The two columns aren't level. So there's a blank at the top of one column. That could happen in either of two ways. One would be if she keyed the first command on the menu – Save Entire Text – without giving any file name at all. I don't think she'd do that, because a careless user could get access by mistake. So what I'd do if I were trying the same thing would be to turn that into a command to erase the sensitive files. The other way would be to give it a file name using only the red function keys.'

'For which we'd need a code?'

'Exactly.'

Keith looked helplessly at the ten red function keys. They were numbered from f0 to f9. 'It could be something like her phone number?'

'Easily. But it could just as easily be a word. After all, it's only a mnemonic. You'd call f0 A, f1 B and so on. After f9 you'd start again at the beginning.'

'And if we guessed wrong we could wipe off exactly what we want to know?'

'Almost certainly.'

Keith glared at the screen, willing it to give up its secret. He was barely aware of an interruption but glanced up to see Hugh Donald accepting a package from a messenger at the door. As he looked back to the screen his eye passed over the novel in which the disc had been hidden. *Poor Jenny* said the dust jacket. And suddenly he knew.

'Got it!' Keith said, so loudly that the others jumped. 'Miss Spalding told her friend that her name was on it. At the time, Jenny only thought that it was an oblique way of saying that she was mentioned in Miss Spalding's will; but in the end that was what made me look harder at this particular book. I think that she used the name Jenny.'

Grenville made a chart on a scrap of paper. 'That would probably mean nine-four-three-three-four,' he said. 'That's if she didn't put any more twists into it. Shall I try it? Forward or backward? Remember, if we get it wrong we may be in for a long delay while the computer gets fed again manually.'

In her photographs, the brilliant Miss Spalding's mouth had shown a sardonic twist. She would undoubtedly have thought of her friend as backward and somehow Keith was sure that such an oblique but caustic comment was in keeping with her character as he was beginning to see it. 'Backward,' he said.

'Try it,' said Hugh Donald. 'It's as good a guess as any other.'

Grenville keyed. There was a flicker and the screen was filled with neat tabulations. 'Eureka!' he cried with unusual joviality.

Hugh Donald leaned forward and switched off the video screen. 'This is for my eyes only in the first instance,' he said. 'Print it, don't even look at the print, just give it to me with the disc and then switch off. What's on here is probably an explosion looking for somewhere to happen.'

While Sheila and Mr Grenville were sent out to take an early lunch, Hugh Donald took the print-out into the inner room, and when at last he invited them to join him he kept it out of view from Keith and Jeremy. It was clear that Hugh had abandoned his passive role and for the moment had taken over, along with the chair behind the desk, quiet command of the proceedings.

'First off,' Hugh said, 'I may as well tell you

112

something which isn't on the tapes and which I'd been hoping not to have to say aloud. My depute was on the fiddle while I was out of the way. The signs are unmistakable. Large orders going to firms on my personal black-list – firms which may not be dearer but which certainly don't give the same value for money as our usual suppliers.'

'What happens to him now?' Keith asked.

'Fired,' Hugh said. 'There's never any point prosecuting. You can't prove that a back-hander passed, although I'm damned sure that he's salted away a fortune more than big enough to make up for losing a job. Unfortunately, he's also refusing to say a word, not even "Good morning", and we can't put any pressure on him because he knows that we can't prosecute.

'Secondly, the messenger brought me three lists – on disc, as you suggested, Keith. One list of the people who might have been glad to see me out of the way. Another of men who bought Armas Alicante sidelocks. And a third list of men who had guns of that make altered.'

'With details of the alterations?'

'As far as we could get them, yes. Not all shops are as meticulous as yours. And I'm afraid that some shops weren't as helpful as they might have been. But it may give us something interesting to compare with what we can get from this print-out. A quick scan suggests that this is far from being a laundry list.'

Hugh took another plunge into the print-out. After a few seconds he whistled.

'The lady had interesting laundry?' Jeremy asked.

'Very. The first part deals with payments into bank accounts. Switzerland, Monaco, Andorra, you name it.' He studied in silence for another minute. 'The deposits seem to correspond roughly with what follows on.

113

They start small, several years ago, and escalate in size and number. No withdrawals. They must total . . . nearly a quarter of a million.'

'She was planning to retire with her girlfriend soon,' Keith said. 'Somewhere warm, where people wouldn't bother them.'

'That figures. The rest seems to be a record of transactions. I suppose she'd need a reminder of what information she'd sold to whom for how much, and this is it. She's used a sort of shorthand for names which isn't always very intelligible. I can read some of them because I knew of the contracts. For instance, CNBR has to be Cuthbertson and Bauer. Others will take some figuring out. But the nature of the deals is clear enough, and, let me tell you, there'll be some red faces if this has to come out.'

'We'll need it as evidence,' Jeremy said.

'Over the dead bodies of twenty or thirty of Aberdeen's most respected citizens,' Hugh said. 'Although, if it's a choice between my good name and theirs, guess who wins. She seems to have started small, passing bribes and taking a cut. Sometimes the bribes went to a firm's buyer, sometimes to an estimator, for information on the bids of rivals. There are some payments here which don't seem to be linked with anything else, so I don't think she was above a little blackmail.' His voice was becoming slower and more absent as his eye raced ahead through the welter of corruption. 'There are one or two deals here which I wondered about at the time. Now I see why one of our contracts for rig maintenance was won by the wrong firm and by a tiny margin.'

Hugh fell silent and scanned on, turning over the folds in the long print-out. Suddenly he looked up. 'Either she was planning to skip out by October at the latest or else she'd gone clean off her rocker. Possibly

114

both. And if she was getting above herself and planning to vanish with her friend to some small Adriatic island, she could have been putting the bite on almost anybody on this list.

'Since about last June, she'd been selling figures to more than one tenderer. As far as I can see, some of the figures were her own guesses, which means that she could pocket the whole of the slush money. It would have blown up in her face as soon as the first tenders were opened and somebody found that he'd got a contract when he thought he'd bought his rivals' bids. Or sooner, if the wrong two men happened to meet and swap a little oil industry scuttlebutt.'

'I suppose that's a motive for murder,' Jeremy said doubtfully.

'Suppose?' Hugh almost shouted. 'No suppose about it. Look at it this way. Some executive pays out ten or twenty K for information which should get his firm a big contract. But he's sold a pup. First, his head's on the block. Second, the story mustn't get out or he's unemployable in the oil industry from then on as anything loftier than tea boy. And, third, he's therefore wide open to blackmail. Oh yes, there's motive for a dozen murders here.'

'It won't be much help if you don't let us see it,' Keith pointed out.

'You go to lunch,' Hugh said. 'Take your time. I've got to do some telephoning. There are a few names I can't guess, and sometimes there's only what seems to be the name of a firm and I don't know who the individuals would be. But give me an hour or so and I'll bloody well find out.'

'You phone from in here,' Keith said. 'I'll sit in the outer office with this.' He took down the Armas Alicante sidelock from the top of a cupboard. 'Our quarry will probably know by now that McHenge has

115

vanished, in which case he may guess that we've got the goods. Jeremy can fetch us a carry-out apiece.'

'I've no cartridges for that thing,' Jeremy said.

'Don't worry about cartridges,' Keith said. 'I've never not had a few in my coat pocket since I was ten years old.'

TEN

There were no alarms. Jeremy fetched food – scampi and chips – and he and Keith ate companionably in the outer office to the accompaniment of Hugh's attentuated voice from beyond the door. Keith found himself half liking the solicitor. He could understand Hugh Donald's contempt for such personal slovenliness and yet sympathise with the other's refusal to let concern over personal appearance deflect him from more important issues such as work, carousal and silken dalliance. And he could sometimes detect wry self-derision in Jeremy's manner.

They avoided the subject of crime. For the moment, the initiative was with Hugh Donald. But when Jeremy visited his flat to fetch beer he was reminded of his woes and thereafter monopolised the conversation.

'That damned woman,' he said on his return.

'Which of many?'

'Your wife's blasted cousin. She's gone and cleaned through my flat,' Jeremy said indignantly, 'and sent all my clothes to the cleaners. I can't find a damn thing. And it'll take years to replace all that carefully hoarded dust.'

Keith looked at him in his dandruffy suit. He thought that the solicitor looked secretly pleased to have found a new mother figure to resent. 'I don't know about that,' Keith said with a perfectly straight face. 'You go in there and sneeze and you'll put it all back.'

Jeremy repressed a snort of mirth and began a querulous speech on the subject of women who wanted to change a man's habits rather than accept them. Keith seemed to have heard it all before. Some of it had passed through his own mind on occasions.

'You've got to remember,' he said, 'that we give way more gracefully than they do.'

Sheila, returning laden with Jeremy's clean laundry, called him a chauvinist bastard.

Mr Grenville's reappearance coincided with that of Hugh Donald, who emerged from the inner office brandishing a much scribbled sheet of typing paper.

'Hail, hail,' Keith said, 'the gang's all here.' He put aside the shotgun but kept it within reach.

'Let's get down to it,' Hugh said. 'This is a list – we'll call it List A – of people who could have wanted Mary Spalding dead.'

'How many names?' Jeremy asked.

'Twenty-two. On disc we have what we'll call List B, people who could have been better off for having me out of circulation. Two hundred and eighteen names, according to my affectionate colleagues.' Hugh sounded a little awed by the number of his ill-wishers. 'Lists C and D, also on disc, comprise people who've bought Armas Alicante sidelocks or put them in for alterations. Could you,' he asked Grenville, 'compare them in the computer?'

'Very easily,' Mr Grenville said.

'Use surnames only in the first instance,' said Jeremy. 'Who knows what variations of initials or Christian names may have been used?'

Mr Grenville keyed in List A and transferred it to disc. He took a few minutes to write a short program. Then he ran it. 'Absolutely nothing,' he said.

'Run it again without List C,' Keith said. 'We've

already guessed that the gun may have been bought in Glasgow, at the shop which was burned out a couple of nights ago. That sale won't be in the list.'

Grenville ran the program again. This time the video screen produced six names.

Bessander.
Craill.
Finlayson.
Harcourt.
McGregor.
Rowan.

'Now compare initials,' Hugh said. 'There could be several men with the same surname.'

Out went Finlayson.

'Still five different men to investigate,' Jeremy said. 'We're whittling it down. But it could still take a lot of time. Do we know the numbers of the guns which were put in for alteration?'

'Not always,' Hugh said. 'Some shops could only find a copy of a receipt. But if we know it it's on the disc.'

The number of Harold Bessander's gun was listed. It cleared him.

'Do we know whether any of the guns were lengthened, shortened or what-the-hell?' Keith asked.

Harcourt's gun had been shortened slightly and had had an ebonite butt-plate fitted.

'Three left,' Keith said. 'Always assuming that he hasn't slipped through the net. The man we're looking for may be on List B, but he may have had the gun altered at the shop which burned. Or he may have said to himself, "Mary Spalding must die. Hugh Donald would be better out of the way. And, by Golly, my friend Charlie Snooks has a gun which is still registered

119

in Hugh Donald's name which he'd sell me for a price and keep his mouth shut afterwards." Or he may have acquired the gun second hand and after the alterations were made to it for somebody else. But before we do a hell of a lot more work, let's take a look at those men. Do you know any of them by sight?' he asked Hugh Donald.

'Yes, of course,' Hugh said. 'If they've got reason to want me out of the road, I've told them the bad news face to face. I know Craill and McGregor. Can't think who Rowan is, though.'

'But have you ever met Craill or McGregor out shooting?'

'Both of them. Henry Craill was invited to the Shennilco shoot last year. J.C. McGregor was one of the guns at a field trial I ran the dogs in.'

'Is either of them a gangling sort of man with a skull-like face, not more than middle aged, careless with his gun and buys the cheapest of cartridges; but a good shot for all that, using an old fashioned, straight armed stance? Possibly left-handed?'

Hugh looked at him sharply. 'You know Henry Craill?'

'Never met him in my life,' Keith said. 'If you'd read my bloody notes you'd have known my description of the man who'd owned that gun.'

'Mr Donald only got that page of notes this morning,' Sheila said.

'And I've been too busy to read them.'

'All right,' Keith said. 'Another not proven. What about McGregor?'

'About my height and as fat as a pig.'

'Put him aside for now. Tell us about Craill. How does he fit?'

'He fits to perfection,' Hugh said. 'He's the managing director and principal shareholder of Subaquagalv. It's a small to medium sized, high technology firm involved in the protection of steel rigs. They're not doing too well at the moment. Craill was desperate to get a particular contract which we'll be letting shortly. The quotations are just in. Craill can give a low price, but it's my own opinion that his process will need renewing oftener than most of the others. Which gives him a good reason to wish me out of the way. I think he was already getting cosy with my depute.'

Hugh dug the long print-out from his inside pocket and unfolded it. 'If I'm reading Mary Spalding's notes correctly—' he went on '—which is far from certain – and if SULV is Subaquagalv, which seems probable, Craill would have been at the front of the queue of those wishing her dead. She was his accountant; if I hadn't already known it, the open accounts on the beginning of her disc would have told me. She seems to have sold the breakdown of his figures to his nearest rival, and a fictitious version of his rival's figures to him. That means that she would have had to be well out of the country by next week when the figures will become. public knowledge.'

Mr Grenville, who seemed to have no interest in the facts once they had been removed from the computer, was absently dusting the video screen. The others were listening intently and struggling to keep up with Hugh's logic.

'What would he gain by killing her?' Jeremy asked.

'Just this. If her duplicity had come to his knowledge, which it easily could, he was in a bind. She would have expected to prepare his final tender for him. If he changed it, she could sell the revised figure. If he put in a tender which she hadn't prepared, she would hear about it, and that would be enough to alert his rival. Her death would not only be retribution for a substantial sum of money which she had tricked him out of, but would give him a clear run to buy his rival's figure from that firm's staff and improve on it by a small margin. And the figures in the tenders, which were opened yesterday afternoon, would suggest that that's exactly what happened. He was lowest tenderer by a few thousand on a bid of several millions.'

Mr Grenville was now using the computer to draw faces on the video screen. Sheila was making a summary in shorthand. The others were still struggling.

'Rowan,' Keith said. 'You must know who he is or you wouldn't have put him on List A.'

Hugh slapped his forehead. 'That's right,' he said. He ploughed back through his notes. 'Here he is. What threw me is that he's a comparative newcomer. According to my colleagues he bought a controlling interest in C & W Foods about a year ago. That was after I'd black-listed them. Their prices were about average but they weren't too careful about quality and you can't afford dysentery on an oil rig.' Hugh switched to the print-out. 'Miss Spalding seems to have taken him for the same sort of ride as she did Henry Craill. Rowan was after a big contract to supply another oil company's rigs and she not only sold him some dud information but she seems to have sold his real bid to more than one of his rivals.'

'Two names, then,' Keith said. 'Craill and Rowan.'

'Hold your horses,' Hugh Donald said. He went back to the print-out again. 'Hold . . . your . . . bloody . . . horses. You know what they say about computers. Garbage in, garbage out. Or to put it the other way, ask the wrong questions and you'll get the wrong answers. Here we are. Six months ago, one of my staff, Tom Marstone, got the boot for leaking our commercial secrets. Leaking them to Miss Spalding from the look of this. He got taken on by one of the firms running supply vessels. He probably faked his references, because she seems to have been blackmailing him for cash and information ever since.'

'He sounds like one of our babies,' Jeremy said. 'What did he look like?'

'That doesn't matter. The point is that about – oh – donkey's years ago a character introduced himself to me at a clay pigeon shoot as being Tom Marstone's cousin. A lanky chap with protruding cheekbones. He had an unforgettable name which, unfortunately, I . . . have . . . forgotten. No, I haven't,' Hugh added suddenly. 'It was Smelly. I remember thinking that if ever there was a case for a deed poll job, or whatever happens in Scotland, that was it. See if a Smelly figures in Lists C or D.'

With some reluctance, Mr Grenville obliterated the face on the video screen, which had begun to resemble his own, and keyed in the questions. Within a second or two, they had the answer. An Armas Alicante sidelock had been altered to fit a Brian Smelly three years before.

'Now, hold everything,' Hugh Donald said. 'I know there's a temptation to gallop madly off in all directions. But today's almost gone and I've got work to do.'

'I also,' said Jeremy.

Hugh seemed unimpressed. 'What's more,' he said, 'we're going to transfer this operation to the Shennilco building.'

'Oh, come on, now,' Jeremy said. 'I can't go trailing out there every time we need a consultation.'

'And I can't spare the time to trail in here,' Hugh retorted. 'But that's not the reason. Use your tiny mind for a minute. We now have three names. Among them, we think, is the name of a man who is prepared to hire Glasgow toughs to break and enter or burn or to kill for him. Don't forget that one of those toughs is running around loose again. We also have evidence, much of which will have to come out if there's a fresh trial, and which will disgrace if not ruin some of the best-paid executives in the oil industry. God damn it, when the news gets around, Harry Snide will probably be rubbing his hands in expectation of boom business! Do you really want all the papers kept here, and ourselves here for most of the time, virtually unguarded?'

Jeremy swallowed noisily. 'My objection is withdrawn,' he said.

Hugh nodded grimly. 'I thought it might be. We can take over a spare office, and there's an entertainment suite on the top floor with sleeping cubicles. They're supposed to be for visiting VIPs or for staff who've worked late, but in fact they only get used after a trade booze-up if somebody's too pissed to go home. The whole building is secure. I suggest that all four of us move in there until we can feel safe again.'

Sheila looked at him. 'Safe?'

'Somebody may very much want to find out how much we know,' Hugh pointed out gently.

That quashed any possible objections.

'That's settled then,' Hugh said. 'I'll get on the phone and see how many cars and drivers we can produce. The drivers will be armed,' he added, 'and I suggest that none of us goes anywhere unaccompanied from now on.'

When Keith returned later to Gregor's Hotel, to collect his luggage and to check out, he was escorted by two armed chauffeur/security guards who seemed to think that they were guarding a Head of State. It would be easy, he thought, to develop a swollen head in such company.

No reporters were lying in wait, but an inspector of police from Strathclyde had arrived to see him. Keith would have sent the guards to pack his cases while he met the inspector, but Hugh Donald had ordered

124

otherwise. One of the men went to do that duty while the other followed Keith into the lounge and took up a strategic position at another table.

Inspector Donelly was a sharp-cornered and uncompromising man with grizzled hair and a look of having seen all that Glasgow could throw at him. He shook Keith's hand but refused a drink.

'Do you usually go around with an armed escort?' he enquired grimly.

Keith glanced at the security man, who was sipping an innocuous tomato juice. No gun was visible although there was a barely discernible bulge on his hip. 'Not usually,' he said, 'but the local constabulary – God bless our boys in blue – decided that, despite Galway being found in my room with a knuckleduster and no explanation, he could be allowed to run around loose. So Shennilco decided to give me a guard.'

'Lucky for him we're not on my patch.'

'I almost hate to tell you this,' Keith said, 'but some of the foreign oil companies have men manning their gates with submachine-guns slung over their shoulders. These oil companies have a lot of clout. When they threaten to move away, taking a few thousand jobs with them, blind eyes get turned.'

'Not on my side of the country they don't.'

Keith was already getting a little tired of the inspector. He decided to introduce a topic which could usually be counted on to reduce any policeman to a state of incoherent fury. 'When the oil boom moves round to the west,' he said, 'you may find that your policy of ensuring that only the criminal is armed and that the law-abiding citizen is at his mercy may have to get modified.'

He paused, but Inspector Donelly came from a tougher mould than Superintendent Munro in Newton Lauder. He refused the bait. 'You said that Galway was

125

still running around,' the inspector said. 'Why didn't you mention McHenge?'

The riposte had been swift and dangerous. Keith decided not to underestimate the inspector. 'I haven't seen McHenge,' Keith said. 'But Galway came to my room and threatened me, and your local brethren didn't oppose bail. So of course he was the one I thought of. What have you brought me from Superintendent Gilchrist?'

'Mr Gilchrist's more interested in what I can take back to him,' Donelly said, but he produced a large, buff envelope. 'You'll find photographs, descriptions and an outline of their m.o.s in there. It's not a lot, but it may encourage you to keep out of their way.'

'I don't need a lot of encouragement. Do we know where they're staying in Aberdeen?'

'Small private hotel. The address is in there. Now, what have you got that might help us with our arson case?'

'Does this go straight back to Gilchrist?'

'Yes. Why?'

'Because the local police have already made up their minds about this one. They're convinced that Hugh Donald killed Miss Spalding and got off on a technicality. That being so, they're not going to give you much help to prove that your arson arose out of the need of a different murderer to cover his tracks. But if you rush into following up what I tell you, my chances of finding the man behind the murder will vanish. And I'm becoming ever more convinced that he inspired the burning of the shop. Give me a few days to find him and your case will solve itself.'

Omitting any mention of McHenge, and therefore of the note from McHenge's wallet, Keith gave the inspector a summary of progress so far. 'So,' he finished, 'we think we may have narrowed it down to a list of three men, each of whom is a perfect fit for motive. Each had access to a gun which matches the one Hugh Donald originally bought.

'But that's three suspects, and we can't even be sure that there isn't another who's slipped through the net. Any chance of your finding a connection between one of these men and Harry Snide?'

'Not a hope in hell,' the inspector said. 'Snide's the most careful villain I ever knew. Nothing's ever in writing. He uses public call-boxes more than his own phone and he has a system of code words which changes regularly.'

'Sod it!' Keith said. 'I was going to ask you to organise a phone call in Harry Snide's voice to Galway – or McHenge. Something like, "The client won't pay his bill. Go round and put pressure on him." At least we'd then find out whether either of those two knows who their client is.'

'Almost certainly, they wouldn't,' said the inspector thoughtfully. 'Knowing how Harry Snide works. And the code words would beat you. But the client might not know that. The voice would be easy enough, rasping and with a strong Glasgow accent.'

Keith blinked at the inspector. He had not yet had time to think the idea through and to have the other take it seriously caught him off guard.

'Look at it this way,' Donelly said, becoming more human. 'You could leak it to each of your suspects that you've passed such a message in Snide's name to those toughs of his and then see who runs to the phone to get the order countermanded.'

'What a devious bugger you are!' Keith said admiringly.

'Aren't I just!' said the inspector. He decided that he was now coming off duty and accepted a large malt whisky.

127

'Would you give me a call if any of Harry Snide's other playmates leave Glasgow, heading this way?' Keith asked.

The inspector thought it over and then nodded. 'That much I can do,' he said.

'And you'll persuade the super to lay off for a few days?' Keith asked.

'Three days,' the inspector said. 'And then you cough up everything you've got. You're holding a lot back, but if I lean on you now I may spoil your working along a line which, for the moment, suits my book. In three days, you tell all, or else. And the super will back me.'

The Shennilco building was a new and glossy structure of many floors, faced in polished granite and bronzed glass, set in an industrial estate which was still in course of development. Keith had once seen an exquisitely dressed duchess picking her way through a farmyard. Among the cranes and chewed earth, Shennilco House gave him the same impression of disdainful skirt-lifting.

In the visitors' suite, the bedrooms were hardly more than small cubicles, but as well and comfortably fitted out as any hotel room. Keith felt at home at once. Tired from his efforts of the night before, he took himself early to his bed and was asleep within seconds.

He was awoken in the small hours by a knock on the door and it took him a great effort to drag himself up the slippery hill to full consciousness.

He found the bedside light. 'Who's that?' he called thickly.

Hugh Donald looked round the door and then came in. Apart from his blue chin he looked dapper in a silk dressing gown and striped pyjamas. 'Sorry to wake you,' he said, 'but I've just had a phone call.'

Keith turned on his back and covered his eyes with his fore-arm. 'Presumably it couldn't wait until morning.'

'Judge for yourself. Following up the last thing you said in Jeremy's office, I had two of our security men go back there to stand guard. They've just caught somebody pussy-footing up the stairs. From the description, it's Galway.'

'Tell them, "Well done!"' Keith said. He began to drift off again.

'Stay awake,' Hugh said urgently. 'There's an important question. Do we hand him over to the police or send him out to join his pal McHenge on the rig?'

Keith fought his way to the surface again and thought about it. ''S a pity to lose the proof of him trying to steal the evidence.'

'That's what I thought,' Hugh said.

'Other hand,' Keith said, 'if we chuck him to the fuzz, he'll have a good story. They'll bail him again.'

'Probably.'

'If we turn him loose and watch him, his actions might tell us whose interests he's looking after.'

'Could be.'

'But,' Keith said, 'he's probably better at watching us than we are at watching him. I'd prefer that our man doesn't have anyone helping him. Inspector Donelly promised to ring me if any more of Harry Snide's boys headed this way. Send Galway out to the rig, and tell them to keep him and McHenge apart. We don't want them comparing stories. You agree?'

'I think so,' Hugh said doubtfully.

'If you only half agree, only send him halfway out to the rig,' Keith said. 'G'night.' He was asleep again before the door closed.

ELEVEN

Keith, as was his habit, awoke early and completely. He showered in the miniature bathroom, dressed and took the lift to the ground floor. A guard directed him to a large dining hall where a small throng of early arrivals, mingled with some departing night staff, was eating breakfast. Most of the table talk was oil industry gossip.

The same guard gave him the room number of the office which had been cleared for them, and Keith found it for himself, a high up and spacious room with a wide view reaching to a forbidding seascape. The computer and their papers were on the long table and Keith settled down.

He was still reading and note-taking an hour later when Hugh Donald came in with another man. 'This is Ken Rothstein,' Hugh said. 'The Old Man's depute.'

Keith got up to shake hands.

Rothstein was a short man with a round, Mediterranean face and a huge moustache. His accent was American but not aggressively so. 'My orders are to see that you get whatever backup you want,' he said. 'So when Hugh asked for a run-down on your short-list of three, we got down to it. Four copies.' He handed Keith a heavy buff envelope.

Keith took a look inside. At first glance, the reports looked remarkably full. 'How on earth did you manage it in the time?'

Rothstein shrugged. 'No great sweat,' he said.

'Personnel still had a fat file on Tom Marstone. And the others do some business with us, so Finance had an angle. We put questions to anyone who'd dealt with them, and the wives of anyone who lived on the same block. Then it was just a matter of an overnight typist taking messages as they were phoned in. I dragged myself in at dawn to edit it.'

'I'm impressed,' Keith said with truth.

'Tell the Old Man, when you meet him later. He thinks I spend my time sitting on my hands. Those notes are no more than general background. Anything else you need, just ask. The wife network makes a good information-gathering machine, we'll have to make more use of it. But for now, I must go. We're meeting one of the union bosses at eleven and I got some preparing to do. Boy, do I!' He smiled wryly.

In the doorway, Rothstein crossed with Jeremy Prather. They exchanged cold nods.

The solicitor placed a heavy package and another envelope on the table and stretched a cramped arm. 'From Tooker. He's been gathering up photocopies of statements and other papers in police hands – I'd rather not know how – plus the photographs which weren't put forward as evidence. His forensic pal was up all night, doing an autopsy on that blasted rabbit. And Sheila says she'll be down in a minute. She's washing out my socks. I didn't ask her to,' he added. 'In fact I asked her not to.'

Keith was already opening Tooker's envelope. He spoke absently. 'It's hard enough to get them to wash your socks,' he said. 'But when a woman's made up her mind to wash them, the only way to stop her's to set fire to them as soon as you take them off. Yours should burn nicely. Well, hullo!'

'Something useful?' Hugh asked.

Keith passed him a photograph. 'Sergeant Tooker's

131

pal got this off the indentations on that note our man sent to McHenge. Some partly legible numerals, which could be a date or time or quantity or almost anything else, and one word. "Winnigstadt". Is it a place?'

'Not that I ever heard of,' Hugh said. Jeremy shrugged.

'Job for Sheila. Let's take a look at these dossiers.'

Sheila made her appearance a few minutes later. 'Look who's here,' she said brightly. A figure loomed behind her which might have been carved in haste from granite. Somewhere within that frame, Keith suspected, lurked a heart of gold, but he had never been able to find it.

'My brother-in-law,' Keith explained. 'Come in, Ronnie.'

'I was half expecting your message,' Ronnie said. He threw himself into one of the empty chairs with a violence which nearly shattered it. 'When I saw in the papers about you putting a bomb under those lawyers, I kenned you'd not manage without me.'

'If you know that much,' Keith said, 'you'll know who I mean when I introduce you to our client and the defence solicitor.'

Ronnie stretched a long arm across the table to shake each man's hand and then collapsed back with a yawn. 'What can I do?' he asked.

'Not as much as I'd hoped,' Keith said. 'I thought the thaw might be here by now. Even so, any evidence on the ground is several months old. You may have to work from these photographs.'

Ronnie thumbed through the batch. 'Photies is no' the same as being able to move your heid and catch the light,' he said. 'Did you fetch me a' the way from Dawnapool for that? I had to dig my way through Strath Oykel yestreen and when I looked round the bloody snow plough was following in my tracks!'

'If you've been driving all night,' Hugh Donald said, 'you'd better go and sleep.'

'I'll do fine for now,' Ronnie said gruffly. 'A stalker soon learns to manage on a few hours now and again.'

'Just listen for a while,' Keith said. 'I'm going to summarise what we know. Then we'll see if you can't add something.'

Sheila opened her shorthand book.

Keith stared at the lowering sky for a few seconds while he arranged his thoughts. 'We could have made a good case against McHenge and Galway,' he said. 'But that would not have cleared Hugh's name, because it could be argued that he could have been their client. So we've put both men into store and thus mucked up some of what might have been evidence against them. Sergeant Tooker reckons that if we can nail the client, the client will shop the hirelings. I hope Tooker's right. If not, we may need all you can get from the ground and from those photographs, Ronnie.

'We've got to go after the man who hired those two. We think, without being sure, that his is one of three names. Craill, Rowan and Marstone.

'Getting enough evidence to determine which of those three is our man, let alone seeing him prosecuted, is going to be about as easy as pulling elephants' teeth. Evidence exists – it always does. But our hands are tied. The police could get search warrants. Jeremy, what are our chances of getting search warrants? Negligible?'

'Less than that,' Jeremy said. 'Nil. We could apply for a Commission and Diligence, but it would have to be in respect of specific items in the possession of one particular man. And even then, he'd be given the chance to answer us in court and give reason why it shouldn't be granted, which would give him the chance to get rid of whatever it was.'

'So much for that, then,' Keith said. 'For the next

step, we must narrow it down to one man. After that, we can look for evidence which will put him in the dock.'

'I don't think we'll get it,' Jeremy said. 'Not with our hands tied as they are. I've been giving it some thought. What we're going to need in the first instance isn't a prosecution but a libel action.'

'We sue somebody?' Hugh asked incredulously. 'The police, you mean?'

'We don't sue anybody. They sue us. Remember the Oscar Wilde case? As soon as we have an identity and a little evidence, we announce very loudly that Mr Craill-Rowan-Marstone caused Miss Spalding's death. And we go on repeating it until he has to start an action for libel. Or if he doesn't, we've made our point. But once he starts an action, the burden's on us to prove that it was true and that it was in the public interest that the truth be known. And, immediately, whatever we've got becomes admissable in evidence and we can get the court's help to obtain more. Access to his bank accounts, for instance.'

The silence while they digested this proposal only lasted a few seconds. Then Hugh Donald nodded. 'We'd better get on with identifying our man,' he said. 'Keith, would you like to run over what we know or can infer about him?'

Keith spread his notes out on the table before him. 'First off, we know that he's been in touch with Harry Snide and through him he hired Galway and McHenge. Money must have passed, and we can look for evidence of that.

'Obviously, he had a motive; but all three of our suspects seem to have been amply provided in that respect.

'We believe that he was on a particular shoot, but the

records are lost and we've no idea who was present that day.

'None of that is very helpful, but at least that's the negative elements out of the way.

'We know that the gun which killed Miss Spalding was for some time in the hands of a man of certain characteristics which I've listed for you. Stringy rather than squat. Eyes relatively wide apart compared with the lower jaw. Careless over his gun and given to buying bargain cartridges. Possibly left-handed. And he may shoot with what I'll call his non-trigger arm straighter than is fashionable nowadays.

'Jenny Carlogie says a man with a deep voice made an upsetting phone call to Miss Spalding. That may or may not have been our man. McHenge thought that his client's voice was deeper than the ordinary. Maybe a woman would notice the depth of a man's voice more than a man would, or maybe not. Make what you like of that.'

Keith fell silent.

'And that's about all we've got, so far,' Hugh said gloomily. 'And if we ever get around to thinking that we've narrowed it down to one man, what do we do then?'

'We try to prove it,' Keith said. 'We start by making sure we've backed the right horse. Probably we set a trap.' He outlined his discussion with Inspector Donelly.

'We haven't much to go on,' Hugh said. Jeremy frowned and nodded agreement.

'Damn all,' Keith said, 'and none of it good evidence. It just shows you how easy murder can be. Hire a pro, pay him with untraceable cash, the deed's done weeks later and the only evidence points to the pro, who needn't know who you are and wouldn't talk about it

135

anyway. There's no link with the real culprit. We're working ninety per cent from motivation, which is the weakest link of all because crimes are very often committed for reasons nobody would have believed sufficient. What we've got so far is mostly nothing trying very hard to pretend to be something.'

'Well, I think it's a lot, considering how little time there's been,' Sheila said hotly. She put down her shorthand book and looked over Jeremy's shoulder. 'From his photograph, that man Rowan looks just the type to be a murderer. That's as evil a face as I've ever seen.'

'It's a snapshot,' Keith said. 'You can't go by that. I'd hate to be judged on the way I come out in snaps. And it's taken from a bad angle and badly lit. I can't even make a guess as to whether that gun would fit him.'

'The photograph shows him as left-handed,' Jeremy said.

'Only that he's holding something in his left hand. Not quite the same thing.'

Hugh had been leafing through Rothstein's folders. 'The dossier describes him as irritable and probably ruthless,' he said. 'On the other hand, I don't remember him on any of the Shennilco shoots after I took over. He's been around Aberdeen for years, but he only came into C & W Foods recently, so we wouldn't have invited him unless there was some earlier connection I don't know about.'

'My choice would be Henry Craill. He's just the shape Keith described, his voice is deeper than average, he's careless of his gun, I remember him being on one of the shoots several years ago and he was using some funny looking foreign cartridges.'

Keith leafed through more papers. 'We've only got one set of dimensions of alterations to a gunstock,' he said. 'That's Marstone's cousin, Smelly. The gun conforms, near enough.'

136

'And Marstone took his dismissal badly,' said Hugh. 'He's a weak character.'

'Guesswork,' Keith said, sighing. 'Wasting precious mental energy. Beating the water with a stick. We've got to narrow it down.'

'One of our stumbling blocks,' Jeremy said slowly, 'is that we don't know who was on one particular shoot five years ago. I've spoken to several men who'd been invited at one time or another, but only one of them could say whether he'd been out that particular day, and he hadn't. Unless they've kept a game book or hung onto their diaries, they just don't know after all that time. But suppose that we got somebody started phoning everybody we know of who's ever been on one of those shoots, asking the question, "Did you ever meet Mr Naulty while a guest of Shennilco?"'

'Go on supposing,' Keith said. 'Suppose that Naulty knows something. Suppose that he's back in this country. We don't know it but the killer does. Might we be provoking another phone call to Harry Snide?'

Jeremy thought for a moment and then shook his head. 'If anybody among them knows anything, we've no reason to believe that it's Naulty. And, obviously, we don't phone our three.'

'True,' Keith said. 'But I've a gut feeling against naming names. I'm beginning to regret mentioning Naulty to the press. And we can't be positive about our short-list. I'd go along with phoning everybody bar our three, and asking, "Who do you remember ever meeting on a Shennilco shoot?" The computer can sort them into groups. If Naulty's name pops up at all, we should be able to pick on the right group. Then we can start to fill out the list for that day. If only one of our three names pops up, we're halfway home. And we can start praying that at least one of the others has a sharp memory.'

'That seems reasonable,' Hugh said, scribbling. 'I'll

get Rothstein to start it going. What else can we do?'

'We can get a whole lot more details about our three candidates. Get Rothstein's team to start again with the same neighbours as before and work on from there to any acquaintance of each of them who isn't so pally that he'd tip off our subject. We want every scrap we can get to fill out the three pictures. Physical description. Height. Character. Previous history. What does he smoke? Where does he shoot and in what style? What gun does he use and how long has he had it? What cartridges and where does he get them? Does he have any connection with Glasgow? I'll make out a list in a minute, but let's have every known fact whether it seems relevant or not.

'Then contact your friend, the OM on the rig. Get him to put some pressure on McHenge. And on Galway, who may know more than we think. McHenge isn't the garrulous type, but he opens his mouth if he really believes his neck's in danger. I want him squeezed dry on the subject of the man he met in the dark. How tall? How did he sound, smell, walk? You know the sort of thing. Oh, and what did McHenge do with the matches he'd scrounged off his client?'

'Can do,' Hugh Donald said. 'Is that the lot?'

'For you, yes. Jeremy, will you chase round the legal and financial network again and see what can be found out about the finances of each of them?'

'I suppose,' Jeremy said.

There had been another paper in Sergeant Tooker's envelope and Keith used a gap in the discussion to run his eye over it. 'I'll be here all day, going through this lot with Sheila,' he said. 'So let me know as and when anything interesting turns up. Well, sod me! That,' he added, 'is an exclamation, not an invitation.'

'Something new?' Jeremy asked.

138

'A long shot paying off. A job for Ronnie, I think. That rabbit was shot after it was already dead. Gassed. Cymag suspected. And there was a myxomatosis sore beside its eye. Ronnie, start with whoever sells Cymag locally. Sales have to be recorded in the poisons book.'

'I doubt that'll help o'er much,' Ronnie said. 'Keepers are aye passing it from hand to hand – that's how it falls into the hands of the salmon poachers.'

'Try it anyway. Or try the chairman of the Pest Control Action Group if there is one. We want the names of everyone who may have been killing rabbits with Cymag around the end of August and who might have passed on a dead bunny to a friend or a customer. Hang on, there may be more.' Keith read on to the end of the report. 'Traces of a heavy, clay soil in the fur. Kemnay's not on clay is it, Hugh?'

'Not by about twenty miles,' Hugh Donald said. 'It's a light, sandy soil.'

'That's what I thought. Also in the fur, seeds . . . Not much help. Nettles and creeping buttercup, both seeding all over the place in August. Stomach contents, predictably grass.'

'You don't seem very surprised,' Hugh said. 'Did you suspect this?'

'I thought of it. There seemed to be a total absence of blood, which needn't mean much. But the photographs of the rabbit showed a blueish trace around the eye membranes, which suggested cyanosis. Anyway, that time of year there's too much cover most places for shooting and too many young underground for ferreting. The other option is to stalk them in the open, but that's better done with a two–two rifle and a bullet hole would have been obvious.'

Hugh was still frowning. 'If the rabbit had been gassed, it'd have had to be dug out,' he said.

'Not necessarily. Sometimes, when you lift the turf

or whatever you used to cover the holes, you find one or two rabbits just below the entrance. Either way, there'd be soil in the fur. And I could see the myxy sore for myself.'

'It'll only lead us to a butcher's shop,' said Jeremy.

'Don't you believe it,' Keith said. 'People have gone off rabbits, even clean ones, since the myxy started. No butcher would take one with sores showing. And finally,' he added, 'could somebody go out to Kemnay and fetch my car? We'll meet again tomorrow morning.'

'Tomorrow's Saturday,' Sheila said.

'Never mind if it's Halloween,' Keith said. 'Let's bring this to a conclusion before Harry Snide sends any more of his boys this way. Or Shennilco's rigs will be getting overcrowded.'

Sheila went to hunt among the Shennilco offices for a large piece of graph paper. For a few minutes, Keith had the impersonal room to himself. He stacked the contents of Sergeant Tooker's parcel but hardly glanced at them. Instead, he stood looking out at the chaos of the building sites nearby, the sparkling countryside beyond and the contrast of the sullen sea, while he juggled with his thoughts. The sun vanished after giving the first new snowflakes a moment of brilliance. Keith was restless and already claustrophobic. He would rather have been outdoors and on the hunt, but he knew that his present job was to co-ordinate.

Sheila brought paper. She also brought coffee and distracting chatter. 'Aren't they taking an awful risk, locking those men up on an oil rig?' she asked. 'What happens when the time comes to let them go?'

'No problem,' Keith said impatiently. 'They're brought ashore and caught trying to stow away on an outbound plane or robbing the Shennilco payroll,

140

whichever suits best at the time.'

'But they'll tell the police where they really were.'

'And they'll contradict each other all along the line. They're being fed conflicting ideas as to which rig they're on, they're seeing different people and hearing different noises.'

'But the police . . .'

'Even if the fuzz believe two men who're evident criminals, they couldn't investigate every rig in the North Sea,' Keith pointed out. 'If they had the men, they wouldn't have the powers. In theory, the rigs come under Aberdeen's Chief Constable, but that's only by courtesy. Strictly, they're in the same class as a ship at sea.'

'It hardly seems right,' Sheila said unhappily, 'to . . . to . . .'

'To seek justice by perverting it?'

'That's it exactly.'

'Those two were doing the perverting,' Keith said. 'While they were running around loose, justice would never be done. We'll salt them away and any other of Harry Snide's boys who may turn up, until such time as we've got justice for Hugh Donald. After that, we'll start thinking about justice for everybody else.'

'I can tell that Jeremy isn't happy about it,' Sheila said.

'No lawyer was ever happy about any positive action. But Jeremy knows which side his bread's buttered. And now,' Keith said, 'let's get down to it. I'm going to make a chart. You go through the statements and put a red line in the margin against anything which wasn't in the precognitions at the trial.'

They worked steadily through the day, interrupted by a steady trickle of information, by visitors seeking to help or to check on progress, or by phone calls in request of further instructions. When Sheila felt hungry,

141

she fetched food for Keith and forced him to eat, under threat of reporting him to Molly.

Keith's chart was divided into three main horizontal bands for the three main suspects, Tom Marstone and his cousin being lumped together, with blank bands awaiting any new names which might be added to the list. The many vertical columns were given over to facts or suppositions. As the squares were filled, Keith ringed any positive, matching evidence in red, hoping that a distinctive pattern would emerge; but, whenever the balance seemed to sway in the direction of one suspect, the next entries would tilt it another way.

In mid-evening, Sheila, exhausted, threw in the towel but Keith slogged on. Rothstein was away and it was left to him to set the night shift of three typists working to make neat dossiers out of the flotsam of paper. Only long after midnight, when he had satisfied himself that order would impose itself on the chaos, did he make for his cubicle, swallow a couple of drams from the hospitality cupboard and fall into bed, only to lie awake until he could coax his mind away from its eternal perusal of a myriad unrelated facts and conjectures.

TWELVE

When the new morning came alive Keith did not revive with it. He slept late and arrived back in the appointed room to find that even Jeremy Prather was there before him. The day being Saturday, the building was quieter than usual; but there was still traffic in the corridors and the lifts were busy.

Keith had pinned his chart to the wall and surrounded it with the available photographs of all four men. Jeremy, Hugh and Ken Rothstein were grouped in front of the display. The room was already hazed with smoke. There were four cigarette ends in the ash-tray beside Jeremy, and Rothstein was puffing a large and expensive looking pipe. Sheila was busily tidying the fresh mass of documentation.

'Any sign of Ronnie?' Keith asked the room.

'Plenty,' Rothstein said. 'Look from the window. You're the whizz-kid at detection.'

'Didn't you hear him come in?' Sheila asked. 'At one in the morning?'

'I went up long after that,' Keith said.

Keith looked down from the window, and indeed the signs were clear to be seen. Ronnie's Land Rover was parked in the middle of the lawn which, Keith had been assured, lay beneath the snow. From it zigzagged a line of uncertain footprints. They paused once and a yellow stain suggested that Ronnie had tried to write his name in the snow, although neither his script nor his spelling had been at their uncertain best. Two other sets of footprints came from the vicinity of the front entrance and the three sets returned in line abreast.

'A pity,' Keith said, 'that our murderer didn't spread as many tracks around.'

'He was singing *The Ball of Kirriemuir*,' Sheila said, 'and getting the verses mixed up together.'

'Then he won't be much help to us for a few hours yet. You aren't supposed to know whether he was muddling the verses or not,' Keith said. *The Ball of Kirriemuir* is a very rude song indeed, much favoured by Scottish Rugby clubs.

'I wouldn't count on any help from him ever,' Sheila said.

'You'd be wrong,' said Keith. 'Sometimes he reminds me of a certain kind of gundog. He may be hard mouthed, a runner-in and incompletely house trained. He may even bite. But give him a line and send him out and most times he'll bring back the bird in the end. I only hope that this is one of the times,' he added, 'because we're getting nowhere fast.'

'We seem to have filled in a lot of the gaps,' Rothstein said gently.

'We have. But the one huge gap between the killers and the client is still very nearly a blank,' Keith said. 'No fault of your gossips, they've done wonders. How did you collect all the financial background, Jeremy?'

The solicitor hesitated and then decided to relinquish the credit. 'By giving your fat accountant friend a thousand quid to spread around,' he said.

'Even so,' Keith said, 'I can't make anything conclusive out of it. If we can't pinpoint our man from what we've got, we'll have to move into the hard phase.'

'Which is?' Rothstein asked.

'Illegal. Burglary and phone tapping. Do you have any contacts in that sort of field?'

'Contacts, yes,' Rothstein said. 'But first you'll have to get it down to a convincing short-list of one. Those activities can backfire, friend. They're less likely to backfire if the party's guilty, because he's too busy trying to explain away what's been turned up to kick up hell over the way it was got. But two, three or even four innocent men, no thank you very much. So let's make sure that we've squeezed every drop out of what we've got first.' He pulled a chair up in front of the chart. 'At a first glace, it looks bad for Mr H Craill.'

'He's got more than his share of red marks,' Keith agreed, 'but some of those are about as speculative as backing horses you've chosen with a pin. I'll give you a frinstance.' Keith took another chair in front of the chart. 'Some answers only came back from Marina Beta late last night, because they'd waited for the proper time to pull up the drill string before threatening to stuff McHenge down the hole.'

'Right,' Rothstein said approvingly. 'Pulling up a drill string costs money.'

'Your men seem to have been pretty convincing. McHenge, and Galway when his turn came, were more than anxious to help. Galway never met the client and couldn't add a thing. But McHenge was positive that he'd smelled cigar tobacco on the man he met in the dark and he was almost sure that he finished the box of matches he'd bummed off the man and that he threw it away in the gulley when he went back up to drop the cheque book. Assuming that that was the matchbox Tooker mentioned – and I can't find another one in the police list – the scorching inside it would suggest a man who shelters the match inside the end of the box. Rightly or wrongly, I think of that as a soldier's habit. Craill had military service so I gave him a red mark, and another for being an occasional cigar smoker.'

'I see what you mean about speculative,' Rothstein

said. 'Most men smoke a cigar now and again. And you get pipe tobaccos made from cigar leaf – Balkan Sobranie in the yellow tin for one. And Rowan's a pipe smoker.'

'Good point. We'd better find out his brand. But,' Keith said, 'would you shelter a match in the end of a matchbox to light a pipe? I thought that it'd be too unhandy.'

'Not with practice,' Rothstein said. 'You turn the pipe over. I do it all the time when I'm outdoors. But let's not fret over details just yet. Run over the main headings.'

'Right,' Keith said. 'Right . . . For starters, the full precognitions, before they were pruned down for use in court, are useful but they mostly don't help us to pinpoint our man. What they do is to help convict McHenge and Galway. As, for instance, Miss Carlogie's mention of the man she saw coming down the gulley. Her mention of the later burglary would probably have been deemed irrelevant. More useful – and I'm surprised that your counsel failed to dig it out on cross-examination, Hugh – is a mention by the cyclist that the man who came back towards the car definitely did not have any dogs with him.'

Hugh Donald sat up suddenly. 'Surely that lets me off the hook,' he said.

'You could have left the dogs in the car for once,' Keith said. 'The good sergeant missed one point. The copper who saw the girl in the shoe shop, where the man whom we can assume to be McHenge bought his calfskin boots, said that the same man had returned later the same day for a pair of green Royal Hunters, the same kind of shooting boots you were wearing the other day. And he took them a size too large for himself. That's why she remembered him.

'The most useful titbits are in the photographs and I

146

suspect that the next judge, if only we can get that far, will take very serious note of the care taken to exclude anything which weakened the prosecution's case. There are some good photographs of the rabbit, showing more clearly the blue colour of the eye membrane and the pattern of pellets on the wall. They should certainly have made your counsel, if he was on the ball, wonder whether the rabbit hadn't already been dead when it was shot.

'Another series of photographs shows tracks coming down the gulley, similar to the one near the murder site. All right, they could have been made the day before; but it wasn't for the police to conceal the information. I want Ronnie to look at them. I get the impression that the walk was quite unlike yours, but he could say for sure.

'Best of all, though, are some photocopies taken from your file with your insurance company, Hugh. You'll remember that they produced one of your policies in court, to back up your ownership of the gun I sold you. But when you changed your policy a year or two later, you filled out another proposal form. You must have taken the number off the gun in your possession again. You quote the number as one–eight–five–four, which doesn't show among the numbers we managed to get from the gunshops. Again, they could have argued that you'd made a slip. They preferred to suppress the information.'

Hugh Donald was looking white. 'But all this suggests malice on the part of the police,' he said. 'They were out to get me, personally. Why would that be?'

Jeremy shook his head, shaking also the ash from his cigarette onto Keith's papers. 'It happens in the normal course of business,' he said. 'The Procurator Fiscal and the Advocate-Depute should only want to show the truth. But the police are evaluated on the basis of the

147

percentage of crimes solved, which really means the ratio of crimes detected or reported to the convictions obtained. So you can see the pressure on them to make sure of a conviction.'

'Whatever the reason,' Rothstein said briskly, 'it happened. Fine. We're making progress. Let's move on.'

'Let's not move on,' Hugh said. 'There's an important point here. Can we use this new material?'

Jeremy Prather scratched his head. (Hugh leaned away.) 'I'm glad you asked that question,' Jeremy said, 'but I'd be gladder if you'd answered it for yourself. The answer, I'm afraid, is a qualified maybe.

'In a libel action, probably not. But, if we could get the Secretary of State to order a re-opening of the case, then yes. But we'd need a lot more than we've got so far. We could apply for a Commission and Diligence, specifying the items we want. The fact that we know of the existence of such statements and photographs might suggest to the police that we already had copies, which would surely deter them from quietly losing anything they were unhappy about.'

'We could always get fresh statements from the cyclist and the girl in the shoe shop,' Rothstein said. 'And Miss Carlogie.'

'If we can drag the police material out into the light of day,' Keith said, 'it'll be a hell of a black mark for that supercilious, arrogant bastard who dragged me into Lodge Walk and told me to lay off,' Keith said. He glanced quickly through his notes. 'We don't seem to have anything fresh about those who attended the Shennilco shoot on Hugh's first day,' he said.

'Soon, I hope,' said Rothstein. 'We've several men to reach yet. Of those we've spoken to so far, several were guests more than once, and even those who've kept game books didn't write down the names of their fellow guests. So, each time, you get a list of the names he remembers but no indication as to which of those names were out on the same day. The task goes on and today being Saturday we may catch more of them at home.'

'Hope so. We need something new. Now we come to the information on the chart,' Keith said. 'Our suspects. We'll take them one at a time.

'Henry Craill's in his early forties, divorced, father of two children but doesn't see much of them. He's described as a rather neutral sort of character. Managing director of Subaquagalv, so he must be making a good screw, but maintenance of his ex-wife and family seems to keep him broke. He lives a quiet life in a flat off Queen's Road, but lady visitors aren't unknown. Occasional, social drinker. Rarely writes a cheque, deals mostly in cash which he withdraws in large amounts at long and irregular intervals. That makes it difficult to guess whether he might or might not have drawn extra to pay blackmail or to settle with Harry Snide, but his withdrawals last August and September seem to have averaged more than his usual. He's a member of a syndicate up Deeside and does a little wildfowling in season. He shoots pigeon and rabbits at other times. He's reckoned to be a slightly above average shot, but very rarely shoots clay pigeons which is the only sure way to judge a stranger.

'His only gun is still an Armas Alicante sidelock, but that could be a second-hander he bought to replace the murder weapon. Sometimes buys cheap cartridges but also reloads his own. Reputed to be careless with a gun; fellow members of the syndicate have spoken to him once or twice about that.

'His ex-wife seems to've had no reservations in speaking about him – I hope no ex-wife ever talks about me like that – and she also produced a good likeness of him.' Keith pointed to a framed photograph of a balding man in tweeds leaning against the back of a car. 'As far as I could judge, he'd fit that gun although he shoots off the right shoulder. Definitely right-handed, for what that is or isn't worth. Not a smoker although he does very occasionally accept a cigar if pressed. He's been on more than one Shennilco shoot. And, other than some comments by his ex-wife about his sexual habits, that's all we know about him.

'Rowan, on the other hand, is right-handed but shoots off the left shoulder because of a fault in his right eye. As far as we know he's never shot with Shennilco. He also is a syndicate member, Donside this time, and in summer he fishes and sometimes shoots clay pigeons well enough to win the occasional competition. Primarily, he's a driven pheasants man. Nobody commented on his style, but being very long armed his hand could be off the fore-end without his arm looking unnaturally straight. Pipe smoker. Aged forty-two. Married, no children and lives in a house in Cults. Described as irascible and inclined to ride roughshod over people. And he looks it.' Keith nodded to a group of snapshots of a dark haired man who seemed to greet each photographer with an individual scowl. 'He certainly buys cheap cartridges, loaded in Taiwan or somewhere.

'Physically, he could fit that gun although the photographs seem to suggest that he's got more chest than I'd expect. That gun might have bruised him on the pectoral muscle unless he adopts a leaning forward stance, which he may well do. He splashed out and had a new Dickson sidelock built to fit him recently, and nobody seems to know whether he still has his Armas Alicante gun.

'He makes money and lives pretty high. He drew out a lot of money between August and November, but he's known to gamble so that may not be significant.

'Then there's Tom Marstone, the only one to have a known connection with Glasgow where he was born and where he visits an elderly relative about once a month. Which means no more than that he had an improved chance of being put in touch with Harry Snide. Aged thirty-two. he lives in a flat, Duthie Park direction, with a young lady whom he refers to as his wife although Shennilco had him down as unmarried when he worked here. His withdrawals from the bank are highly irregular, probably because his lady friend is a freelance artist who makes her income in large lumps but not very often. So it's impossible to say whether he's still on the take and whether he's been hiring thugs as well as making the contributions to Miss Spalding's retirement fund which showed up on the disc. He doesn't shoot, but he's a compulsive smoker of anything that burns.

'His cousin, Brian Smelly, fits the physical description adequately. He used to buy cheap, foreign cartridges but gave them up. Shoots vermin, wildfowl and clay pigeons and is reckoned a first class shot. Shoots off the right shoulder. He usually has about six or seven guns, to suit his different sports, and he's always chopping and changing – nobody so far remembers seeing the Armas Alicante sidelock since last summer, but summer's when he'd be using it for pigeon and rabbits; he's the sort of man who'd go wildfowling with a magnum and have several trap guns to suit the different disciplines. He seems to have been a guest of Shennilco but, it's thought, not until very recently. He paid some cash into his bank during September, which could have been the sale of any damn gun, not necessarily the murder weapon.

'And,' Keith said, 'that's about the lot that's any use. We have a great deal more gossip which may come in handy if and when fresh questions arise but, for the moment, those seem to be the relevancies. And, as far as legal proof goes, it could still be any one of them, if it's not somebody else.'

Somebody sighed. There was a dispirited silence while a girl from the typing pool brought in a note for Rothstein and another for Keith. The others stared at the chart, hoping that the words and squares would form themselves into a face.

'No help here,' Rothstein said. He crumpled the note and threw it on the floor. 'We've reached a man who was on the shoot with Naulty. He remembers everybody. Where he can't remember a name, he gives a description or some other identification. It's clear that neither Rowan nor Craill nor Marstone's cousin were among those present.'

The silence was longer and even less happy. Hugh Donald broke it. 'Right back to square one,' he said sadly. 'You did your best, Keith, but it's no go. I'd better start looking for another job.'

'If you're a quitter, you'd be better in another job,' Rothstein said. 'But you may care to remember that, before we underwrote this investigation, we had you sign an agreement to stay with the company for five years. The company'll decide whether you go or not. And we're not dead yet. There's other ways guns get passed from hand to hand.'

'True,' Keith said. 'But the traffic in second-hand guns is constant and unrecorded.'

'Well, don't give up yet,' Sheila told Hugh. 'I still think it's Mr Rowan. Even in the good photograph, he looks as if he'd kill his mother if she annoyed him.'

'You may even be right, honey,' Rothstein said, 'but, around here, you got no vote.' Sheila reddened but compressed her lips in silence.

Keith jumped in quickly. 'I'd like to plump for Craill myself,' he said. 'After umpty years of fitting guns to men and men to guns, I can usually put my hand into the rack and pull out the one which will fit a customer. And without thinking about it. The one looks like the other, if you understand me. All three men look like that gun, near as you can judge from photographs, but Craill looks more like it than Rowan or Smelly.

'But, on balance of probabilities, I've got to say that Rowan's our boy. Even for a good shot, that gun would be unsuitable for either of the others; but it could suit a driven game man who goes in for high pheasants. Either of the others would have had the chokes opened out, to give a better chance at snap shots at closer targets.

'Also, when I heard about his new gun, I phoned a friend at Dickson's. That note was a telephoned message from him. He's only just managed to look up the details of Rowan's new gun. Heavily choked in both barrels, and the same angle at the butt as the murder gun. To my mind, that clinches it.'

'You could be right or you could be wrong,' said Rothstein, 'but you sure as hell don't have enough to persuade me to commit us to illegal surveillance.'

'Shit!' Hugh Donald said. 'Begging your pardon, Sheila. But for Christ's sake, Ken! Before you'll sanction a real investigation, you want the sort of information only that sort of action will bring out. Morton's bloody fork!'

Rothstein shrugged. 'That's the way it is,' he said. 'The Old Man's prepared to go all the way within reason, but there's a limit.'

'Agreement or no agreement,' Hugh said very quietly, 'I can't take much more of this.'

The silence came back. Keith could hear sounds on the floor below, traffic outside and the cry of a gull as it hung on the wind.

'We do know one more thing,' Jeremy said suddenly.

'Something which we haven't resolved and which might pin it down. Our man passed a note which carried an impression of the word Winnigstadt. We still don't know what it means but it sounds German. Craill's firm uses a German process,' he added.

'We'll follow that up,' Keith said. 'But we need something new. A fresh fact. Or a *deus ex machina*.'

'Would I do for that?' enquired a voice from the doorway.

THIRTEEN

'Bloody unlikely,' Keith said.

The Land Rover eccentrically parked below might pass, on its better days, for a machine, but anything less like a classical god than his brother-in-law Keith had yet to see. Ronnie, who was unshaven and wearing a dirty old shooting coat instead of a dressing gown, was clearly in the terminal stages of hangover.

And yet there was about him an air of placid satisfaction quite unlike the jubilant pride which usually marked a successful quest. It took Keith only a few seconds to recognise the symptoms. His brother-in-law had scored with a lady.

Ronnie was quite unabashed at his deplorable condition. 'You'll just need to do the best you can,' he said, 'because I'm all you've got. I came down to tell you not to beat your brains out. Yon mannie Rowan's your lad. Christ, you needn't have fetched me a' the way through a blizzard from Dawnapool to tell you that! I could ha' telled you o'er the phone if you'd asked me and gi'en me what you'd got.' Having said what he'd come to say he broke off and blinked around the room. 'The one time I need coffee,' he said, 'and the first time I've seen this room and it no' full of the stuff.'

Sheila started to get up and then sat down again. Duty called, but curiosity called more loudly. Keith sympathised. 'Coffee's the reward you get after you've told us all about it,' he said.

'Ah, ye bogger,' said Ronnie, but he lowered himself carefully into a chair. 'It was this way. There's a pest control action group right enough. The chairman's a retired general who's laird of a great skelp of useless land on the wrong slope of the hill, up by Forest of Birse. He put me onto his grieve, who does the real trauchle.

'There was nae doubt I'd found the right man. That grieve knew all that was going on in Grampian and half Tayside, and what he didna' ken he got out of the minutes. I'd fetched along a map and he'd soon marked off the areas where there'd been the myxy around just then. And he ticked them off by whether or no they used Cymag around those parts. For rabbits I mean, no' for salmon.

'After he made some phone calls, to check whether this laird or that would let a poisoned or myxied rabbit go off the place, and also crossed out those he was sure were on sandy soil, we'd narrowed it down to four patches.

'He suggested I speak wi' a big agricultural contractor who does the drilling on a whole lot of farms and who'd ken for sure where you'd find the heavy clay. He phoned the man's home for me and found that, the time o' year being quiet, the man wasn't working but was taking his dinner in a posh hotel in Banchory. The grieve came wi' me, just to be sure I found the place.'

'I bet,' Keith said.

'We had a dram or two with the contractor mannie,' Ronnie said. 'An' he told us that, out of the places we'd picked, the likeliest was an area around Ellon which is worked by a pair of trappers.

'I set off again – the roads was terrible – and I never did find one of those men, but I caught the other at last, in the back room of a wee pub near Oldmeldrum, and he could speak for the both of them – after I'd loosened him up with a few more drams.

'He said that they mostly sold snared rabbits to the butchers, but they're made to use Cymag when the infestation's bad. And the shops'll no' take a rabbit that shows signs of the myxy. They're not so keen on gassed ones either. So those were sold to a hotel which goes in for traditional foods – venison and the like of that.'

Keith felt his stomach in revolt. 'You mean,' he said, 'that a respectable hotel would buy rabbits which had got myxomatosis and had then been gassed with cyanide?'

'Why not?' Ronnie asked reasonably. 'There's neither of them does any harm to the meat. I eat them myself,' he added, as if that settled the matter.

Keith had once seen his brother-in-law eat a cowpat for a bet, so he was less than reassured. 'It's revolting,' he said. 'And I'll bet the Environmental Health folk would do their bloody nuts. But never mind. Get on with the tale.'

'You're o'er pernickety,' Ronnie said. 'Anyway, I was off on my travels again and it was still snowing on the higher ground. I was glad I'd got the Land Rover. I was in four wheel drive the most of the way.

'I found yon hotel at last, and had another dram for the cold before I spoke to the woman that does the buying of the game and suchlike. She'd been at the desk but she was just coming off, so we had something to eat together.'

'And to drink,' Sheila said.

'That was later. By then, I'd barely had enough to wet my lips. I'd no need to show her the photies of Rowan, she knew the mannie fine. She'd never seen any of the other three afore. But Rowan had been to stay at the hotel for the fishing or shooting, and he'd been to

157

dinner there with some businessmen just a day or two before the lady was killed. One of the men had had the rabbit pie, and afterwards Rowan spoke to her. He asked for the recipe and he bought just the one rabbit out of the hotel's freezer although the recipe called for more.'

Hugh Donald put back his head and looked at the ceiling. 'That's more like it,' he said. 'Now we're getting somewhere.'

Sheila slipped out of the room.

Keith was frowning. 'There's got to be more,' he said.

'Not a damn bit,' Ronnie said. 'Not what you're after.'

'Then how did you get so snockered?'

'Och well,' Ronnie said bashfully. 'The lady was glad enough to get a lift home with her bicycle, and she kens fine how to make a man feel good.'

The penny dropped at last. 'Bicycle?' Keith said. 'You don't mean that that was Miss Carlogie?'

'Aye, that's the woman. A gran' body. To look at her, you'd think her a dried up old towdie, but you'd be wrong. I'm thinking I'll be back that way again.'

Jeremy Prather was laughing. 'You said you'd got everything she knew,' he said to Keith.

'I dined at the hotel the other night,' Keith said plaintively. 'I had the rabbit pie.' But it came to him that any harm would have been over and done with by now, and he shrugged. 'They do it in milk, with bacon and mushrooms,' he said. 'It was delicious. But what I meant, Ron, was that you couldn't have told us this over the phone. You didn't know it.'

'That's right,' Ronnie said. 'It was only when I walked in the door just now I heard you talking about Winnigstadt. That'd've been enough to put me onto the

158

mannie Rowan who, you told me yourself, supplies food to oil rigs.'

Keith fought aside an urge to tear his own hair or Ronnie's. His brother-in-law often had that effect on him. 'Stop blethering,' he said, 'and tell us. Do you know where Winnigstadt is?'

Ronnie grinned unbeautifully. 'This time of year it's all over the place,' he said. 'Winnigstadt's a winter cabbage. Aabody kens that.'

'We can't be sure that the note was made in connection with business,' Jeremy said. 'He could have been buying seeds for his garden.'

'Rowan's the only one of our suspects who has a garden,' Keith pointed out. 'The others live in flats.'

Ken Rothstein got to his feet. 'That's good enough,' he said. 'I'll go and see who we know who can tap phones.'

On the evening of that same day, Keith was back in the lounge of Gregor's Hotel with a small and ostensibly sociable party.

It had been a hectic afternoon. Jeremy Prather had vanished with Sergeant Tooker to meet some disreputable acquaintance of the latter who could arrange technical but highly illegal surveillance of Mr Rowan, his house and his telephone. Hugh Donald and Keith had gone in search of the most willing and suitable person to lay the bait.

Ronnie, after an hour's sleep, had joined two of Shennilco's security men in keeping watch on the Rowan house. Sheila, protesting that she wanted to see some of the action and that, the day being Saturday, her time was her own, had wanted to join the watchers, but instead had been put in charge of the liaison arrangements which would be necessary if and when Rowan cast up at some suitable place.

But they had encountered one of their rare strokes of luck. The first message intercepted by the wire tap had been an arrangement by Rowan to meet a friend for a drink at Gregor's during the evening. This had allowed the team a respite and, more importantly, had enabled the party to assemble convincingly in advance of Rowan's arrival.

Ronnie, as the unknown face, had been detached for shadowing duty and was yawning in a corner of the bar. Jeremy had asked to be excused – his help, he said, would be more valuable in rescuing the others from the consequences of actions which would undoubtedly stray far beyond the bounds of legality.

Keith and Hugh Donald occupied a corner of the lounge. They were accompanied by Sheila and a pretty but silent typist from Shennilco, and by Mr and Mrs Handford. Mr Handford, an executive of middle rank from Shennilco's Finance Department, was along as a mildly interested spectator. His wife, a statuesque woman of well-preserved middle age, was very much involved. She had provided many of the details in Rowan's dossier and, although she had tried to be impartial, her mistrust of the man had been evident. In particular, she had damned his treatment of his wife. Keith had wondered whether she might not be a classic example of the woman scorned and so might refuse to move against him.

Mrs Handford had soon put his mind at rest. 'Emily would be better off without that bastard,' she had said briskly. 'He's more than capable of all you're thinking. And if he's innocent – which I suppose is possible – there'll be no harm done.'

Keith had arranged the seating with some care, in a position where anyone heading for the bar must see them. Mrs Handford was to be the only person to meet

160

Rowan's eye, but he would see Keith and Hugh in profile.

They had arrived early and Mr Rowan was late for his appointment. They nursed innocuous drinks while conversation faltered and died.

Mrs Handford took the bull by the horns. 'Suppose,' she said, 'that he believes me. He thinks that two baddies are after him. What do you expect him to do?'

Keith had been bending his mind to the same question. 'I expect him to get on the phone to Glasgow in a hurry, to get the dogs called off,' he said. 'You see the little man sitting near the public phones, nursing an attaché case? That case is full of electronic gear, and he swears he can record both sides of any conversation. I just hope he's right.'

'If I were in Hector Rowan's shoes,' the lady said, 'and if I were guilty, I'd take a room for the night and phone from there. What then?'

'We've got the telephonist in our pocket,' Hugh said.

'And if he changes hotels and does the same?'

'Then we've got to hope that their telephonist fancies a fistful of fivers,' Keith said.

'Suppose he stops at a call-box in the street?'

'We'll have to get our little man close in a hurry and hope for the best,' Keith said. 'But it's not likely. If you had two Glasgow killers after you, would you stop in a lighted phone booth on a dark night?'

Mrs Handford started to speak, broke off and stared over Keith's shoulder. 'There he goes,' she said.

'Did he see us?'

'He caught my eye and he gave you a good looking over.'

'That's good. You move into the hall now, but stay where he can't see you. My brother-in-law – the man who looks like a hairy tree trunk – he'll fetch you if and when Rowan's on his own. Otherwise, try to catch him

161

on his way out. You know what to say?'

'I have it off pat. I heard one of you on the phone, using a rasping voice and a Glasgow accent and saying that Mr Rowan wouldn't settle his debt and is to be dealt with. As a friend of his wife, I thought that he ought to know.' She rose and swept out.

They had only sat in tense silence for a few minutes before she was back and taking her seat. 'His friend hadn't turned up yet,' she said. 'I gave him the message.'

'How did he take it?' Hugh asked quickly.

'I couldn't tell. He just grunted. What will you do if he doesn't bite?'

'We'll be in for a long slog,' Keith said, 'and with the odds against us. Now we just sit tight. Ronnie will give us the nod if he moves.'

Mrs Handford nodded. 'We'll sit it out with you,' she said. 'But, now that I've done my bit, perhaps I could have a proper drink?'

Keith got up again. 'Of course,' he said. 'Anything you like. You've earned it.'

He left an order with the waiter and then crossed the hall to the gents. Excitement, and restricting himself to the weakest beer, had put a strain on his bladder. Relieving himself at one of a row of empty stalls, he fell into deep thought and was only vaguely aware that he had company until a hand between his shoulder blades pressed him forward and a voice spoke in his ear.

'Try your tricks on somebody else, Mr Calder.'

Rather than wet his feet, Keith put one hand out to the wall to balance himself. He glanced over his shoulder and without surprise saw Rowan's face looming angrily above him. He recognised the rodent-like teeth and peevish lips in the photograph, but he could now see what the inadequate photograph had hidden, that the eyes were wide-set over narrow jaws.

'I don't know what you mean,' Keith said.

He felt the other's impatience through the hand in his back. 'Don't give me that,' Rowan said. Over the smells of germicide and air freshener, Keith smelled a blast of stale pipe smoke. 'Sending the Handford woman to me with fatuous tales won't get you anywhere.' Keith thought that the voice was a few tones deeper than his own. He wondered whether to give Rowan an elbow in the gut. The man's absolute confidence suggested that he had been in touch with Harry Snide recently and knew that McHenge and Galway were out of touch. He hoped without much hope that the phone tap had caught that call.

'What a pity!' he said mildly.

'As for tapping my phone, you know that's illegal. I could have you for that.'

'It's less illegal than conspiracy to murder,' Keith said.

Rowan snorted disgustedly. 'You can't prove a damn thing and you know it,' he said. He leaned more weight against Keith's back.

'We can prove corruption and conspiracy,' Keith said. His position was becoming acutely uncomfortable. 'We broke the code on Miss Spalding's discs. And the information's safely stored, so don't bother sending your friends after it again.'

'I should worry! I can prove that whatever I've done is normal business practice in this industry. The only thing that bothers me is having it known that that bitch had me for a sucker.' Rowan paused and then rushed on. 'If you'll suppress the discs, I can supply you with evidence against the two real killers. How about that?'

'We've enough evidence against Galway and McHenge,' Keith said, 'but it's no use to us on its own. We're out to clear Hugh Donald, and it could still be presumed that he'd hired those two instead of doing the

163

job himself. Sorry, my lad, but it's you that's for the high jump.'

He felt the hand between his shoulders quiver with fury and he braced himself for a physical assault. He reminded himself that he must not kill the man, even in self-defence, or Hugh Donald's name might never be cleared.

Rowan hesitated again, but the fury in his mind did not find an outlet in simple violence. Instead, he leaned forward and spat copiously into Keith's ear. Then, as the door opened and two men clattered into the echoing room, the pressure eased and he was gone.

Keith washed his ear carefully and returned to the hall of the hotel. It was his turn now to quiver with fury.

He stood in the hall for a minute, to get his breath, recover his temper and plot the next moves in the game. If he reported the failure of their trap while he was still angry and unprepared, Hugh would be sure that his battle was lost.

And yet, they had taken a step forward. They could now be sure that they were in pursuit of the right quarry. Now the real grind could begin. He would lose the joy of the chase in the chore of guiding hounds.

Manpower would be needed, to visit every gunsmith in the country, to research every minute of Rowan's past life, to monitor his comings and goings and to follow up every tiny lead which might or might not lead anywhere. More traps must be set in the hope that Rowan would slip and convict himself. And, eventually, if they went on long enough and if Shennilco's budget could stand the strain, somebody would say the right word. The lucky break which they so much needed would arrive, provided that someone recognised that word instead of letting it slide away again into limbo.

Just one piece of real evidence, he thought. Give them

that and they could rock Rowan off his pedestal or persuade the legal system to do it for them. But where could it be? With professional killers interposed between the real culprit and the victim, how in God's name could guilt be proved?

His reverie was interrupted by the appearance of the hall porter at his side. 'It's Mr Calder, isn't it, sir? There's a caller on the line for you, from overseas. Transatlantic, I think.'

'I'd better take it,' Keith said. It was probably only a customer referred from the shop.

'You can take it in the last booth,' the hall porter said.

Keith ducked under the plastic hood and picked up the phone. 'Hullo? Calder here.'

The voice on the other end was unmistakably Scottish. 'Mr Calder? I'm calling from Houston, Texas. I just flew in from Caracas. My daughter in Ayr phoned me this morning. She tells me that yesterday's paper had an item in which you said you wanted to get in touch with me. My name's Naulty.'

'Mr Naulty, I'm delighted to hear from you,' Keith said. 'Can you shed any light on how the gun which Hugh Donald bought in Newton Lauder passed into other hands? You were with him at the time of the purchase, I think.'

'That's right,' said Naulty's voice. 'And I can tell you exactly what happened. Mr Donald kindly invited me to a shoot a few days later. Afterwards, I noticed that we seemed to have swapped guns. I intended to contact him about it but, before I could do it, the opportunity arose to come out here. Somebody who heard that I was going abroad made me an offer for the gun. The two guns were virtually identical, so I just accepted the offer. The purchaser was a man named Rowan. I explained to him about the accidental exchange and he said that he would see Mr Donald about it, but it seems that he

165

didn't bother. . . . Is that what you wanted to know?'

'That's exactly what I wanted to know,' Keith said. He found that he was looking through the open doors into the bar where Rowan, in expansive mood after working off his spleen, faced him. Rowan lifted his glass in ironic salute and Keith beamed back at him.

'Was the gun still as standard?' he asked into the phone.

'I'd only had the gun a month or two,' said Naulty's voice. 'I was going to have the chokes opened up and the bend altered – the gun shot slightly high for me – but before I got around to it, my time in Scotland was over.'

'Would you make a statement to that effect and sign it in front of a notary public?' he said into the phone.

'If you like. But I'll be coming over to see my daughter very soon.'

'That's fine,' Keith said. 'But let's have the notarised statement anyway. We wouldn't want anything to happen to you, would we?'

FOURTEEN

Keith was on the phone to Molly. 'I'm coming to get you,' he said.

He heard her giggle, all the way from Aberfeldy. 'I seem to have heard you say that before,' she said. 'Promises, promises. Can you get here? The Devil's Elbow's still blocked.'

'I'll get through somehow.'

'Have you solved the problem of how to prove Mr Donald's innocence?' Molly had been kept at least partly informed through Keith's occasional, guarded phone calls.

'Yes.'

'How?'

'Brilliantly as usual,' he said.

'Oh, you! Never mind, you can tell me again. But Keith, from what I read in the papers there were some Glasgow toughs after you.'

'That's all finished,' Keith said. 'The first pair vanished—'

'Keith, you didn't . . .?'

'They're due to make a miraculous reappearance shortly, and in highly incriminating circumstances,' Keith said. Molly's anxiety would not be satisfied with so bald a statement, so he went on. 'Meantime,' he said, 'a friend in the Strathclyde fuzz phoned to warn me that Harry Snide had sent off a bunch of really hard cases in this direction. I asked him to have the word dropped in

Harry Snide's ear, quite truthfully, that several kilos of statements proving his client's guilt were on the way to the Attorney General, the Secretary of State and, under embargo, the newspapers, so that Harry's chances of getting paid for any further work were less than good. The men were back in Glasgow the same day.'

'Thank the Lord for that!' Molly said. Keith could hear the relief in her voice. 'And will Mr Donald get a fresh hearing?'

'No doubt of it,' Keith said. 'Prather said at first that they wouldn't re-open the case because Hugh hadn't in fact been convicted of anything. But we've tracked down some large sums of embezzled money, and the litigation required for its recovery will be impossible without the whole story being proved in court. Add the fact that we can prove conspiracy to murder against somebody else and there's no way they can avoid a fresh hearing.'

But it seemed that Molly's interest was in Hugh's prospects rather than in the intricacies of his case. 'How's Sheila getting on with Mr Donald?' she asked.

'It's Jeremy Prather she seems to be setting her cap at,' Keith said.

'That lawyer with soup stains all over him?'

'That's our boy. She's cut down his smoking, and now she's trying to get him to go jogging with her.'

'Whatever can she see in him?' Molly asked.

'He's efficient in his way,' Keith said, 'once you get him going. He put together a superb set of papers for the Secretary of State almost on the nod, and now he's already got the nuts and bolts of preparing the brief for Hugh's counsel well in hand. That's how I can get away.'

'He may be efficient,' said Molly's voice, 'but he isn't a catch to compare with Hugh Donald.'

'That's for Sheila to worry about. And, by the bye,

the woman who shared with the murder victim has a good chance of a fat reward and she's spending it on a holiday in the Greek islands and – guess what – taking your brother Ronnie with her.'

'I thought that she was supposed to prefer the company of other ladies,' Molly said.

'She seems to fancy a change. God knows, women seem to fall for the most extraordinary men at times.'

'Don't we just!' Molly said.

It took Keith several seconds to think of a suitably crushing retort and by that time Molly had disconnected. She knew when to make sure of the last word. Keith put his tongue out at the phone and went back to his packing.

XXXIV